91-08

Adrenaline
High

Adrenaline High

Christine Forsyth

James Lorimer & Company Ltd., Publishers
Toronto, 2003

First publication in the United States, 2003

James Lorimer & Company Ltd. acknowledges the support of the Ontario Arts Council. We acknowledge the support of the Government of Canada through the Book Publishing Industry Development Program (BPIDP) for our publishing activities. We acknowledge the support of the Canada Council for the Arts for our publishing program. We acknowledge the support of the Government of Ontario through the Ontario Media Development Corporation's Ontario Book Initiative.

The Canada Council | Le Conseil des Arts
for the Arts | du Canada

ONTARIO ARTS COUNCIL
CONSEIL DES ARTS DE L'ONTARIO

Cover design: Clarke MacDonald

Canada Cataloguing in Publication Data

Forsyth, C.A. (Christine A.)
    Adrenaline high

ISBN 1-55028-793-1 (bound)   ISBN 1-55028-792-3 (pbk.)

I. Title.

PS8561.O6966A74 2003   jC813'.54   C2003-904206-5

James Lorimer & Company Ltd., Publishers 35 Britain Street Toronto, Ontario M5A 1R7 www.lorimer.ca	Distributed in the United States by: Orca Book Publishers, P.O. Box 468 Custer, WA USA 98240-0468 Printed and bound in Canada

*To Katy Stephen, my high-school confidante.
Special thanks to Abigail Bimman and
Kat Mason for your insight and advice.*

Chapter 1

"I will not not." I snapped my *Barbie* lunch-box closed to punctuate my answer. My mother, the English teacher, says good punctuation makes all the difference.

"Good," said Abigail. "Then we'll all meet at my locker after our last class."

Kat, who had been checking out the boys across the cafeteria, turned her attention back to the table. "I thought D'Arcey just said she wasn't going."

"I said, 'I will not *not*.' Two 'nots' make one 'will' or 'shall,' if you wish." And then I stood up because I always like to make some kind of dramatic gesture after every comment. Punctuation!

My two best friends, Abigail and Kat, were still just sitting there. Kat was rolling her eyes. Okay, I'll admit that at times, I, D'Arcey Dufresne, high school junior and human dynamo, can be quite exhausting to hang out with. But most of the time it's fun.

A little wacky, maybe, but certainly never boring. Just a little imagination and some good props make all the difference. Did I mention punctuation?

So, like I said, I'm D'Arcey Dufresne, age sixteen. I live in Toronto, which is great because there's lots of shopping and cool stuff to do. I have lots of friends, but Abigail and Kat are my *best* friends because everybody needs at least one best friend. I've known Kat the longest. Her older sister was my babysitter and she used to bring Kat along. I picked Abigail for a best friend in Grade Six. She's really smart and I like having a friend who gets *all* my jokes. Kat's smart too, but she just doesn't pay attention all the time.

I like to imagine that a camera follows my every move. That way, I think twice about doing something that makes me look like an idiot. And we all know that looking like an idiot in front of other people is just about the most humiliating thing that could happen to a teenager. Of course, it's possible that what's humiliating to you is just good punctuation to me. Which may explain Kat's rolling eyes.

It is my lifetime ambition to be a television news journalist. That's also why I want to be comfortable in front of a camera. Not just one of those shiny heads that stand around and talk after all the excitement dies down. No, not me. Excuse me, not I. In about ten years, you should look for me in war-torn wherever, dodging rocket-launched grenades and getting the scoop of the century. Make that millennium. Century is so last decade.

I have been hooked on cable news since I was born. Really. My father, the history teacher, is absolutely obsessed with the news. I mean, can you imagine living in a house where your parents yell at you for turning *off* the TV?

Anyway, that's how I got interested in the investigative journalism biz. My favourite correspondent is a very serious-looking brunette with glasses like me. I think brunettes are way more serious-looking than blondes, don't you? Not that I don't respect blondes. Kat and Abigail are both blondes. You should see Abigail's hair. It is so thick and curly that it looks like she's carrying a big yellow tent on her head. And Kat has lots of long, wavy hair. They're both so much taller than I am that when I stand between them I look like I'm standing under the golden arches.

Here's a career tip for other short people like me — television news correspondents are usually only seen from the waist up, so it doesn't matter how tall you are. You can even wear jeans to work if you want to.

So, there I was, still waiting expectantly beside the table. "*Fête accompli*, ladies. Party's over."

Although I was born in Toronto my family roots are in Penetanguishine, Ontario, where a large percentage of the French-speaking population is actually related to me. I don't know that much French, only what my grandmother taught me, but I like to use it as often as I can. Or German, or Italian or any language. Toronto's great for picking up foreign languages. In my neighbourhood we have lots of Italian-Canadian families, and Greek-Canadian families and, well, you get the picture. My foreign language skills will come in handy when I travel the globe as a foreign correspondent slash investigative journalist slash celebrity interviewer slash talk show host.

"*Fête accompli*," I repeated. My friends, through long experience and French class, know that "*fait accompli*" means, essentially, a done thing. But according to my mother, language is a living thing and I'm all for changing an expression to give it a new lease on life. Our daily lunches are a party or *fête* according to the "DuFrench" dictionary, and this *fête* was definitely over.

The thing I'd agreed to do with Abigail was going to be fun. I was looking forward to another trip to the thrift store. It is absolutely one of my favourite places to shop. When you only have a measly allowance and the paltry tips from waitressing to spend on clothes and cosmetics, your money goes a long, long way at thrift stores.

The three of us had a major project to prepare for our Media Studies class and Abigail had chosen to recreate the early days of live television drama. She was in the market for fifties-style clothing for her cast. We were going along with three other girls in the cast to select our costumes. I didn't have a lot of time because I couldn't be late for my part-time job.

"Why aren't the boys coming?" Kat asked. "I thought there were boys in your show."

"The boys aren't coming?" I said, feigning shock and horror by putting the back of my left hand to my forehead. Abigail playfully slapped my hand away.

"They wouldn't be caught dead thrift shopping. Besides, they're just going to wear regular pants with white shirts and white socks. That's what men wore in the fifties. And borrow cardigan sweaters from their dads or their grandfathers. Everybody's grandfather has cardigans."

"I don't have a grandfather," I said, my hand rising once again to my forehead.

"Oh stop it," said Kat. "You have the coolest grandmother in the world. You don't need a grandfather."

"Or a cardigan," Abigail added.

"You are correct," I concurred, "Mémère is quite possibly the coolest old doll on the planet. I mean, who else would dare name a restaurant *The Liver Spot* and serve liver for breakfast, lunch and dinner?"

"Like, what's up with all that liver? I mean liver — yuck! Do *you* actually eat liver?" Kat held her nose throughout her comment, making me and Abigail hoot with laughter.

"Yeah, I do. And don't you dare laugh. It's good for you. Full of iron and vitamins and stuff. And if you don't look at it when it's raw, it's not so bad. But it kind of smells. I think that's what the onions

11

are for. To mask the smell. Why are we talking about liver? We have class in about 30 seconds."

I snatched up my lunchbox and used it to point to the cafeteria doors. "Barbie says *andalay*," I announced. That's "walk this way" in Spanish.

* * *

The shopping trip was a raucous, giggling success. Each of us found a perfectly hideous outfit we couldn't wait to wear. The colours clashed spectacularly. I found a pair of red Capri pants for $2.99 and a yellow hand-crocheted cardigan that looked like it was a bunch of those poodle toilet paper cosies all sewed together. Both would go brilliantly with my absolutely favourite red, yellow, white and turquoise striped tank top. I couldn't wait to show Mémère.

Three evenings a week, I wait tables at *The Liver Spot*. It isn't hard work because dinner time at the restaurant only lasts from about 4:00 p.m. until 7:00 p.m. Most of Mémère's regulars are seniors and have eaten and gone by 5:30 p.m. That leaves an hour and a half to clean up and chat with Mémère.

Her restaurant is located on a really busy section of St. Clair Avenue. It's painted a cheerful yellow, like the yolk of an egg. Every table is covered with a sparkling white tablecloth and Mémère's diners always eat off of good china and use the silver cutlery she provides. Mémère fashioned her restaurant after a European bistro because she thinks it reminds her many immigrant customers of home.

When I finally got there, the only customer left was Mr. Plawicki. He's one of Mémère's "Three Squares," regular customers who eat breakfast, lunch and dinner at the restaurant. We think Mr. Plawicki is Mémère's boyfriend, which she denies. The fact that Mr. Plawicki was still there after dinner meant that he was angling for some alone-time with Mémère, or he was so completely senile that he forgot he's supposed to go home and sleep between dinner and breakfast.

I was sitting on one the bar stools sipping my eleventeenth cup of coffee of the day. Mémère hoisted herself onto the stool beside me. She's a little shorter than me, and I'm short. But she's a fair bit wider and, in her colour-coordinated yellow apron, she looked like an extremely cheerful fire hydrant.

"I got a whole set of bathroom covers like that for a wedding present," said Mémère on seeing my cardigan. "Five pieces, I think, for the seat, the tank, toilet paper, Kleenex and oh, I don't remember. But it was pink."

"Eeyuck," I said. "That's gross." Except, I actually said, "Dat's gross" to mimic my grandmother's French Canadian accent. Mémère knows when she's being teased, but never complains. She simply cannot pronounce "th." It comes out as "d." She never says "h" either. It was years before I realized her brother's name was Hubert, not Ubert. And tell me if this makes any sense — she had another brother whose name was Earl. You know what she called him? Hurl. What's up with that?

"You should come thrift shopping with me, Mémère. They've got lots of cool stuff."

"No, no. I already have all my clothes," Mémère said.

"How can you 'already have *all* your clothes'?"

"I'm old. I don't need new clothes. I have clothes in every style since 1945. They come back in style, I wear them. They go out of style. I put them away." It was quite true that Mémère's closet was a treasure chest of vintage clothing. I've been raiding it for years.

"Don't you like to wear something new when you go out with your boyfriend?" I said, looking at Mr. Plawicki, who was reading the same paper he'd started at breakfast.

"He's old too. *He* doesn't remember what *I* wear. *I* don't remember what *he* wears. It works good. Besides, he's not my boyfriend. He's my liar."

"Mémère, call him what you like, he's still your boyfriend. Although I must say if he's a liar, I'd dump him if I were you."

"He's not *a* 'liar,' he's *my* 'liar.' He takes care of my will and my real estate." Mémère said, exasperated.

"Oh, I get it, he's a lawyer. Mémère, I think maybe when you introduce him to people you should let him tell them what he does."

"Ha, you think *my* accent is bad? He's Polish."

"Yeah, but I still bet he doesn't go around telling people he's a liar."

"*Tant pis*. Enough. Go home and do your schoolwork, ma fille, and maybe someday you can go to university to become a liar too."

* * *

I didn't have any homework to do that night because I'd done it at *The Liver Spot*. When I got home, my parents were sitting on opposite ends of the couch, reading newspapers. The television was tuned to a news magazine show, although no one was watching.

"I'm home," I announced. Their heads snapped up simultaneously. "Hi honey," they said in unison. They looked like bookends — two short, brown-haired people wearing glasses with a stack of papers between them. I guess you could say I have my mother's looks *and* my father's looks. I definitely got my hazel eyes from my mother and my grandmother. Hazel isn't an actual colour because there isn't a crayon that comes in that shade. When I was a little kid, I wrote and complained to the crayon people.

"I'm going to take Rooter and Jake for a quick spin around the park," I told my parents.

"It's almost dark, D'Arcey. I'm not comfortable with you being in the park at night."

"Oh, Dad. It's only eight o'clock. Besides, we're the only people in North America not watching the finale of 'Who wants to win a million bucks by stabbing other people in the back?' So who else is going to be out there?"

"I'll go with you, D'Arcey," my mother replied.

"Cool. C'mon Rooter, let's get you saddled up." I headed for the back door with Rooter, my awesome two-year-old chocolate Lab right behind me. Jacob Two Two, my cat, heard the sound of the dog's feet on the kitchen floor and sped through the family room on his way to join us.

My father, who likes most cats, frequently complains that looking at Jake nauseates him. I will admit that Jacob is quite an unusual-looking cat. One side of his face is grey tabby like the rest of him, but the other side is a demented patchwork of black and white. It's like he has two halves of two different faces, and it's really difficult to look at him directly. It doesn't help that his eyes are two different colours. But that's why I picked him. Because he was different. And I named him Jacob Two Two after the title character in one of my favourite stories.

"We're almost out of T-R-E-A-T-S," I called from the pantry while my mother finished with whatever article she was reading. "I'm putting them on the Franz."

"Franz?" I heard my father say.

"The list, Pierre. She's putting them on the grocery list."

"Then why doesn't she just say 'list,' Selina?"

"Because she's studying the lives of the great

16

composers and righ s reading about Franz Liszt."

"Well, that explains ept why she calls a list a Franz. think I get it."

Educating your parents

* * *

After my walk in the park, wh
my mother pick up the dog poo,
less from the kitchen and strolle
So far, I had failed miserably in n
convince my parents that we need a
line. My older brother, Derek, who
year at the University of Waterloo, ne
phone when he was home. He seeme
where to be and when, by some sort o ...ental
telepathy. And my parents rarely talk on the phone
for long, so if I can't have a line of my own, at
least I'm not being constantly hounded for
monopolizing the phone. It's my nightly ritual that
I use a feature I'm quite sure my parents don't
even know we have — three-way calling — to
conference-call my friends.

But first, I turned on my webcam and entered our
private chat room. At the same time, I logged onto
three different instant messenger programs and
polled around the universe for other friends who
were online. In one hand, I held the cordless and set
my customized "D'Arcey News Network" micro-

phone in its stand beside the webcam. It's really just an old karaoke microphone but I've added a cardboard box around the handle, near the top and pasted on the "DNN" logo that I made on my computer.

Abigail and Kat were already online. The little video boxes showed them in front of their own computers, talking on phones wedged between their ears and shoulders and clicking their keyboards frantically.

"My dad got me a video of some TV dramas from the fifties," said Abigail. "Everybody looks so old. I don't know any of the actors. They must all be dead."

"We could search them online," I suggested.

"Yeah," said Kat. "Give us some names."

"Paul Newman," said Abigail. "That sounds familiar."

"He makes spaghetti sauce now," said Kat.

"Yeah, but he still makes movies," I said.

"Like what?" said Kat.

"Spaghetti westerns."

"You're kidding!"

"Duh! Don't you watch vintage TV?"

"No, and neither do you, D'Arcey," said Abigail. "You don't have digital TV. None of us has digital TV. That sucks. I'd be so much smarter if we had digital."

"Right, like everything you know you learned from reruns."

"Shut up, Miss Media Superstar. You know, if you don't present an idea for your Media Studies project soon, Mr. Carswell is going to assign you something really stupid," Abigail said, sounding quite smug because her project had been enthusiastically endorsed by our Media Studies teacher. Neither Kat nor I had presented our ideas yet — Kat because she didn't have an idea, and me because I had too many. Abigail is the one person I know who can be relied on to do everything on time. I don't think procrastination is in her dictionary. I enjoy taking a little extra time to think things over, myself. Which, if you look at it my way, isn't procrastination at all.

"Well, I have news for you. I've decided. And it's going to be brilliant." I added my favourite computer sound effect of hands clapping.

"So, tell."

"So, no, eh. You'll have to wait, like the rest of the world, until class tomorrow. All will be revealed."

My computer sneezed to announce a new message. "And now, a word from our sponsor," I said, cuing the croaking frogs. "Gotta go. That's Mama Selena instant messaging me from the computer downstairs. She wants the phone. See you in the morning."

Chapter 2

"Are you ready, D'Arcey?" The words had barely left Mr. Carswell's lips and I was on my feet, marching confidently to the front of the classroom. "Evidently so," he said.

The class twittered, but unfazed as usual, I plugged the laptop I'd borrowed from the computer lab into the borrowed projector and signalled for Abigail to dim the lights. The screen filled with the image of a painting of barren rock and twisted pines.

"It was a dark and stormy night," I began. The class groaned. "And Hubert Deschamps was late." On the next slide, the pines were replaced by a photo of young man in an old-fashioned suit and hat, holding a machine-gun. That got their attention, especially the boys. "There was money to be made by moonlight." Back to the groans. The man melted away and a sleek vintage wooden speedboat with lots of chrome appeared. Now all the boys "ah'd" in appreciation. Figures. "So Hubert set out under cover of darkness with a boatload of whisky and nothing to keep him company but his trusty gun."

Man, did I love this! I sure had their attention. Now for the kicker.

"Only the boat came back." I paused for maximum effect, "Hubert, the whisky and the gun were never seen again." I finished my presentation with a brilliantly created image of an empty grave superimposed over the powerboat.

Allowing this spooky image to sink in, I waited a full 30 seconds before signalling to Abigail to turn on the lights.

There was enthusiastic applause from the boys.

"That was very interesting, D'Arcey," said Mr. Carswell. "What do you intend to do with this story for your project?"

"I'm going to make a docudrama. I will, of course, direct and star in it. I'll investigate and solve the mystery of Hubert's disappearance once and for all."

"That's a tall order, D'Arcey. Is this a true story?"

"It is," I replied, "Hubert Deschamps was my great-great-uncle. My grandmother's uncle on her mother's side."

"When and where does this story take place?"

I'd done a lot of research for my project online and at the library besides listening to Mémère's stories. "It takes place in Windsor during the

American Prohibition, in 1932," I said.

"During Prohibition," Mr. Carswell jumped in, "selling and drinking alcohol was illegal in the United States."

"But not in Canada," I added. "At least not at the same time. We had Prohibition too, for a while, and that's how my great-uncle got his start in the bootlegging business. During the First World War there wasn't any liquor being made in Canada because they were really busy making war stuff, so Great-Uncle Hubert made his own and sold it. He was only nineteen."

"Bootlegging," said Mr. Caswell, in his Mr. Dictionary voice, "is the illegal distribution of liquor."

"Anyway," I said, waving my arms for attention, "people were drinking their faces off in the States and because they were drunk all time, they didn't go to church, so the government decided to make it against the law to make and drink alcohol. So the gangsters, like Al Capone, smuggled it in from Canada. And when Prohibition started in the U.S., in 1920, Great-Uncle Hubert took his speedboat and moved to Windsor, which is just across the river from Detroit. My grandmother says that he and his gang stole whisky from the distillery there and took it to Detroit in the boat. He did it for a long time, almost ten years, and then he disappeared."

"Well, D'Arcey, I have a couple of problems with your project. First, the reasons for Prohibition were complex and you will need provide a more complete background. More importantly, illegal guns and stolen alcohol are not themes we like to glamorize in high school."

Needless to say, I was prepared for Mr. Carswell's objection. I'd discussed my project with my mother, who also taught in the Toronto high school system, and she'd raised the same objection.

"But sir, there's a moral to the story. He led a life of crime, and he died because of it. I just want to show that crime doesn't pay. It never did. And it never will. Not then, not now." Okay, so maybe that was laying it on a little thick. But sometimes I find that excessive sincerity weakens the strongest resistance.

"Well," said Mr. Carswell, after pausing to consider, "in that case, we could let it through, but I want to see your script before you go too far."

Beside me, Abigail snorted and I shot her my "shut up" look.

"Donkey shoes," I said to Mr. Carswell.

"Pardon me?"

"Donkey shoes. That's German for 'thank you.'"

Mr. Carswell looked a little puzzled by my free-form pronunciation but he let it pass and said, "All right. You've got a project, D'Arcey, now how many people do we need for your cast?"

"Like I said, I'm going to star in it myself, as the investigative journalist, and I'll probably just play most of the parts myself. I'm very invested in this project."

"But D'Arcey, how are you going to play your uncle?"

"Oh, make-up, costumes, wigs, stuff like that."

"We've got a whole class full of people appearing as cast members in everyone's project. You should include some of them in your film."

"But Mr. Carswell, that's the problem, they're in a whole bunch of videos already and they're going to be too busy and I have to go up north to shoot a bunch of it and that would mean taking people with me and …"

"You're going to shoot this on location?" asked Mr. Carswell.

"Yeah, the boat's up there and Mémère, my grandmother, actually has some of Uncle Hubert's clothes and things."

Hands shot into the air, as all the boys clamoured to be cast in my docudrama.

It didn't take me long to realize I'd just hit the casting jackpot. "I don't think I'm going to mention that his gun disappeared too," I whispered to Abigail.

* * *

Kat slid a cafeteria tray onto the table, knocking the contents of my *Teenage Mutant Ninja Turtles* lunch-box into a disorganized mess into my lap. I waited patiently until Kat had unloaded the tray and disposed of it under the table before arranging my tiny plastic floral arrangement, miniature can-

24

delabra with real candles, itty bitty tablecloth, napkin and real silver cutlery in the correct order on the table.

My thermos remained tightly sealed in front of me. "I'm going to wait for A.B." I always pronounce Abigail's initials in French, as "Ah Bay." Don't you agree it was very clever of the Bermans to name their daughter Abigail so that her initials and my short form of her name were so congruous. In fact, I'd told them so when I first met them and they'd looked at me oddly ever since. Parents. Just when you think they're being clever, they become completely obtuse.

When Abigail finally appeared, I greeted her with an enthusiastic "Ah Bay, say!" To which Abigail replied "Duh Ay." And that was our signal for lunch to begin.

"Ninja Turtles? Have I seen that one before?" said Abigail, tapping my lunch-box with a fork.

"No," I said, "I got it at the thrift store on the weekend. It's mint." My collection of lunch-boxes is quite amazing, if I must say so myself, although my mom complains about how much room it takes up in the basement.

"Do you realize you're the only person in this entire school who still carries a lunch-box?" asked Kat. "Doesn't that embarrass you even a little bit?"

"As if," I said in reply.

"Nothing embarrasses D'Arcey," added Abigail. "Nothing embarrasses her and everything embarrasses me. My mother embarrasses me, my sister embarrasses, even when I see someone doing something on television that's embarrassing I get embarrassed. God, I wish I had your self-confidence."

I shrugged a classic French shrug. It is true that I am quite confident about most things, but I am sometimes bothered by bouts of self-doubt. Sometimes, but not often. What I do have in spades is decisiveness so that while everybody is waffling about what to eat, what to do, what to buy, I make up their minds for them and forge ahead. Except when I'm procrastinating for creative purposes.

"So, are we in your docudrama?" I knew Kat was dying to know.

"Yeah, are we?" added Abigail.

"Like, I don't know. There aren't that many girls in the story. Maybe just Mémère when she was young. And the beautiful young correspondent who follows the unfortunate Hubert on his date with destiny."

"Doesn't he have a girlfriend?"

"He doesn't need one. He has the beautiful young correspondent following him around."

"Eyew. That's weird. He's your great-great-great-uncle or something and your gonna be like his girlfriend," said Kat.

"No, I am not like his girlfriend. I'm just the beautiful young correspondent. One should not infer anything else."

"So it's just you, somebody playing Mémère and a bunch of guys?" asked Abigail.

26

"Oh, I think we could slip an extra moll in there," I said to tantalize them.

"A what?" Abigail and Kat asked together.

"A moll," I replied. "That's what you call a gangster's girlfriend."

"Why?" said Abigail.

"I don't know. Probably because they didn't have much to do all day so they hung out at the mall." I was pretty sure that they didn't have malls in those days, but it sounded like a reasonable explanation. At least Abigail and Kat bought it.

While I poured out my Friday soup, which is always tomato, Abigail started on her sandwich. She took one bite, put the sandwich down and turned to me.

"If the beautiful young correspondent follows Hubert on his date with destiny, wouldn't she see what happens to him? And then there wouldn't be any mystery to solve."

"Hmm," I said, slurping soup from my monogrammed silver spoon. "Yes, that could be a problem. That would certainly take the drama out of the docu."

Kat, having eaten her lunch in what appeared to be one big bite, piped up with "Maybe she was at the mall with the moll."

"Maybe she was at the hospital helping the moll get a brain transplant," I said and went back to slurping soup with intense concentration.

Kat, with nothing left to eat, resumed scanning the cafeteria for boys.

Abigail leaned over to Kat and said, "Good one."

In a rare period of silence, we sat. Clearly, Abigail was ruminating on another flaw in my plan because she added, "You know, D'Arce, while you're in the hospital with the brain transplant moll, you might want to ask about bionic arms."

"Whyzzat?" said I, recommencing slurping.

"You're gonna direct this thing, right?"

"Yeah."

"And you're gonna star in it, right?

"Yes."

"And you're gonna film it, right?"

"Yes, yes, yes. Next question?"

"And are you gonna have your DNN news microphone too?"

"Yes, yes, yes to the tenth power."

Abigail poked Kat to ensure she had her attention too. "Well, who's gonna hold the camera?"

My spoon stopped of its own will, a fraction of an inch from my gaping mouth. After a moment's hesitation, my arm resumed motion, my mouth opened, the spoon entered and soup was sucked. I punctuated this event with a nasal "hmmm" that slid down a ten note scale.

"Kat," I said, daintily wiping my mouth with my monogrammed napkin. "Have you ever considered a career in cinematography?"

"Hmmm," replied Kat. "I'm seeing dark, I'm seeing stormy, I'm seeing night."

"Cool. Tomorrow, I'm bringing the video camera.

We can start getting comfortable on camera," I said. "I want you to shoot my every move."

"Oh yeah, like I'm going to sit through class with a camera glued to my face so I can enjoy watching you chew your pencil."

"Okay, never mind. We'll just work on the 'tone.'"

The ever-practical, and somewhat sly, Abigail interrupted to make one final point. "Who's going to play Hubert? Shouldn't we start working with him right away? For tone," she added.

"I know, I know," Kat practically shouted. "Get Derek."

I groaned. "Derek isn't in our Media Studies class. Derek isn't even in high school. Derek is in university, and, in case you haven't noticed after all these years, my brother is a complete jerk."

"He is not." Abigail and I had long stopped teasing Kat about her infatuation with Derek. For Kat, Derek was the absolute pinnacle of boydom. And even if he never appeared to know her name, he was unfailingly polite and always said hello in reply to Kat's fawning, adoring — and rather embarrassing — greetings.

"I have an idea," I said. "Tomorrow, we'll hold auditions. I'll hold the mic, you'll hold the camera."

"What do I hold?" said Abigail.

I grinned. "Your tongue, missy."

Chapter 3

Kat complained that her arm was getting tired, and griped about how much her eyes hurt, as our day of videography wore on. Abigail and I had taken our turns with the camera to relieve Kat but I could tell, despite her complaining, that she was actually excited to be the official cinematographer. Mostly because she kept telling us that we were doing it all wrong. She said that shooting inside the school didn't give her enough creative opportunities but at least it was helping her get used to the camera, while she learned to focus properly and experimented with the zoom feature. She was relentless with that zoom.

"No zits!" I commanded.

"What?" said Kat.

"I can hear the zoom, and anybody can see the lens moving in and out. You're barely three feet away. You're going to make me look like a great big zit."

"A zit with a very nice microphone," added Abigail. "And a matching sweater."

"Shut up." Admittedly, the breakouts on my forehead make me quite self-conscious and any attempts to cover them up with make-up only make it look like I have pinky brown pebbles on my forehead. I seriously considered bangs just to hide them. Honestly, puberty started three years ago. Enough with the zits.

"It's not that bad," said Abigail. "At least your zits come and go. Mine are permanent."

"Did they have zits in 1930?" asked Kat.

"I don't think so. I've never seen any pictures of people with zits in Mémère's photo albums."

"Maybe they just don't show up in black and white pictures," said Abigail.

"Hmm," I said, getting another brilliant idea. "Let me see that camera. I think it shoots in black and white."

While I fiddled with the camera, Kat and Abigail got bored and wandered off down the hall. The school was all but deserted. Classes were done for the day, which was good for filming because the halls were usually so crowded that it would have been impossible to keep nosy parkers out of the shots. Actually, it was creepy quiet, which was a little unnerving, so I hummed a little of Liszt's "Hungarian Rhapsody" while I cycled through the camera options. I stopped humming briefly to catch a breath. The click behind me was so loud I nearly jumped out of my skin. I swung

31

around but no-one was there. Still, the unexpected sound seemed to hang in the air.

Five metres down the hall, the double doors to the school auditorium were closed. Students aren't allowed in there without a good reason, and there were no practices that day. Of course, a custodian or a teacher could have been in there. But custodians usually made a lot more noise and a teacher probably would have asked me what I was doing hanging around the hall after school.

A mystery noise. And there I was with a video camera in my hand. How convenient. I slinked over to the doors and carefully pulled down the latch, pushing the door open a crack. The auditorium appeared quite empty in the gloom, but then a movement near the stage caught my eye. I caught a glimpse of a lone student. I recognized her. She was one of the new girls in our year. Darned if I could remember her name. She rarely spoke to us, meaning she was either shy or stuck up — I thought the former because she didn't seem to have any special friends of her own and hung around the edges of various groups.

I closed the door as gently as I had opened it and nearly leapt into the air when I turned around to find Abigail and Kat standing directly behind me.

"Whassup?" asked Abigail.

I held a finger up to my lips to shush them while I waited for my heart to slow down. They became impatient by the time I finally beckoned for them to follow me as I opened the door again.

"Hey, I didn't know the auditorium was open. We're not supposed to …" Kat stopped when I gave her my "D'Arcey-says-don't" look.

Here was a mystery begging for investigation. I led the other two into the auditorium with stealthy steps, filming the whole time. Fortunately, it was carpeted so we made virtually no noise at all. Just inside the door leading backstage, I halted to listen. We all held our breath and we could hear only the gentle whirr of the video camera in the narrow corridor.

Soon the sound of rustling paper rewarded our stealthy maneuvers. Behind the stage we came up on three small dressing rooms and a prop room. As we made our way backstage I noticed that the doors to the dressing rooms all stood open as usual because they always needed airing out. During school productions it could get pretty rank in there. The late afternoon light from a small window high up on the wall barely reached the floor. In the dimness, a sliver of light peeked out from under the prop room door like an arrow leading us on. It was the only other place to hide. Usually, the prop room was locked because of the valuable items stored there. Over the course of my three-year drama career, I'd visited the prop room many times. It was spacious and filled with metal racks.

I grasped the knob and twisted gently. The handle didn't turn, but my exertions forced the door open slightly until I could see the heavy tape holding the lock back.

The rustling of paper stopped but I could sense the presence of another person. I wondered if she'd heard us too. Either way, she was trapped because there was only one way out and the three of us standing right there. I didn't want to scare her silly but I was totally pumped.

I was going in. I leaned against the door to hold it ajar and used my free hand to point first at Abigail and Kat, and then to the floor. I wanted them to wait there while I investigated.

Turning left inside the door, I kept my back to the wall as I scanned the rows of props using the camera. I felt just like a real investigative videographer, hunting down a story. Provided the girl wasn't hiding among the set pieces, I planned to pan the camera down each aisle in turn until I found her. I hadn't decided yet what I was going to do when I did.

The narrow camera viewing angle cut out my peripheral vision completely. Searching this way was fairly stupid, considering that you couldn't really see anything that wasn't directly in front of you. I nearly screamed out loud when a man's face filled the viewfinder.

I backed hastily out of the row, lowering my camera. Once I was able to see both sides of the racks, I realized that the "man" didn't have a body. A painted bust of Elvis stared back at me, sitting on a shelf at my eye level. My heart was pounding so loudly by now that I was only dimly aware of noise in the farthest corner of the room. Elvis's pink lipstick distracted me.

In the last of the four rows, I found the evidence. A rumpled sleeping bag, backpack and lots of fast food wrappers were piled against the wall. Adrenaline coursing through me, I scanned with the camera. I was disappointed nobody turned up. So who was making the noise? A library ladder led my eye up the wall to the upper shelves.

Truthfully, the excitement was making me lightheaded, or maybe squinting through the eyepiece skewed my vision because the shelving unit on my left appeared to flex and sway. With a horrible screech of metal on metal, the unit toppled. I leapt back into the safety of corridor at the end of the rows as all heck broke loose.

Items crashed to the floor as the end unit forced the next one in the line to fall over.

"A.B., Kat, quick, get in here!" I screeched still clutching the camera. "Help me hold this thing up! Hurry!"

I pushed my back against the tilting unit while more items crashed to the floor. Kat and Abigail joined me, and with our combined exertions we halted the slide. Carefully, I eased my weight away from the shelves. Kat and Abigail held it up together. I peered between the shelves. The girl hung, trapped between two units. She was crying. I felt like all kinds of bad for causing her to injure herself.

"We'll get you out of there," I assured her. "Are you hurt?" She didn't answer me.

"I said, are you hurt?" This time I put my face cautiously between two shelves to get a closer look.

"No. Maybe a bit," came the reply.

The girl was sprawled across the fallen unit. Somehow she'd stopped herself from falling down between the two. No foothold existed and each time she moved, it pushed the two units together, forcing the one Kat and Abigail were holding up to tilt more.

"I'm going to pull you off," I said. "Give me your hands."

From behind the shelves, Abigail suggested, "Take her feet, D'Arce, that way she won't come down face first."

"Okay, did you hear that?"

"Yeah," the girl mumbled, waggling her feet around to the edge.

"Hold on, I'm going to take this real slow," I announced. Then I grabbed the girl's feet and started pulling gingerly. She helped by wiggling herself over the edge. I heard Abigail and Kat grunting with the strain on the other side. Her legs were hanging down over the edge now so I grabbed the girl by the waist. Her butt was in my face at this point. Not exactly my idea of a news-worthy rescue. I pulled.

"Ow, watch my boobs," she said.

"I'm not touching your boobs," I barked, letting go. She rocketed to the floor, landing in a heap at my feet. She sat up, with her arms crossed tightly across her chest and tears staining her face. With the extra pressure off the shelf, Kat and Abigail tried rocking it back into place.

"Wait a minute," I said. "We'll try to push this one back up first. Can you help me with this?" I asked the girl. After a lengthy pause, she rose and grasped an upright shelf. We pushed and pulled until I could wiggle between to get some leverage. Eventually, we raised the unit and forced it upright. "They should bolt those things to the wall," I said.

"They probably weren't expecting anybody to climb on top of it," Abigail observed, coming around join us. The three of us stared at the dishevelled girl.

She faced us, arms still crossed over her chest. We must have been pretty intimidating. She was not more than an inch or two taller than me but the other two towered over her.

"I'm D'Arcey Dufresne, this is Abigail Berman and that's Kat Morgan."

"I know who you are."

"Oh," I said stupidly, still wracking my brain for the girl's name.

"You don't know my name, do you? I'm in most of your classes. I sit behind you in Chemistry."

"I do so know your name," I said, playing for time to remember it.

Abigail said, "You're Zania …"

And I finished, "You're Zania Thomas and you used to go to Central."

"Yes, now will you please just go away and leave me alone," said Zania.

"Sure," I replied. "Except I'm just a little curious why you're hiding out in the prop room." I couldn't resist focusing the camera on Zania while I waited for her reply.

"Turn that off!" huffed Zania. "Just leave me alone. It's none of your business."

"Oh, I think it is our business, 'cause we're in the middle of a great big mess and I've got the film to prove it." I was sorry I'd said it before I'd shut my mouth. Her face crumpled and fresh tears started.

"Sorry," I said, "I didn't mean that."

Zania wiped her face with her sleeve. "Look, I'm serious. This isn't something you want to get involved in."

My antenna went way up. It sounded exactly like something I wanted to get involved in. Let's face it, I can't resist an interesting story and here was one standing right in front of me. I wasn't leaving.

"Don't be so hard on her, D'Arcey," said Kat.

"Okay, okay. I'm sorry, Zania, I apologize. We're not going to rat on you. But seriously, you can't stay here, because if we saw you, somebody else is going to see you eventually and they may not care who knows you're here."

Trying to be logical and persuasive at the same time takes skill.

"Look, Zania, obviously you're hiding from something, and maybe we can help you out, without telling anyone you're here. Like, how long have you been here? Do you have enough food?" Abigail asked gently.

That comment hit home because Zania started

crying again. I put the camera down and fished in my pocket. I reached around in front of Zania because she'd turned her back on us. I dangled a clean handkerchief in front of her face.

"What is that?" Zania asked.

"It's a handkerchief," I replied, wondering what planet this kid came from.

She took it and blew her nose. When she was finished, she finally turned to face us, holding the damp handkerchief up in front of her.

"You don't want this back, do you?"

"Naw. I got a million of them. My Mémère gives them to me for Christmas and birthdays."

"Do they all have this little 'D' on them?" Zania asked.

"You bet."

"Weird."

"Hey, *you* think *I'm* weird? Who's living in a closet with the Seven Dwarfs?" I asked, picking up a Dopey lawn ornament off the floor. "So?" I resumed my quest for the story. I really wished I had my microphone, but I'd left it in the hallway.

"Listen, I'm telling you, you really don't want to get involved. Just go and shut the door behind you. And you can go right on ignoring me in class. I don't care."

"Look, we're sorry we ignored you, okay? We won't do it anymore," I said, sounding every bit as lame as I felt.

"So now you're my new best friends?" said Zania bitterly, finally showing some spark.

Y

39

I knew this wasn't the moment for a witty comeback, but witty comebacks are my specialty and for a moment I was actually lost for words.

"No," I said, still in my lame-mode.

"Yeah, I figured," Zania said with obvious contempt.

"What I mean is, yes, you have no reason to trust us." I was sinking fast. "So we can't be friends until we show you that you can trust us." I let my words settle in before continuing. "Like I said before, you can't stay here because somebody's going to find out and then what happens?" Without waiting for Zania to reply, I just kept on talking. "You need someplace to stay where nobody would ever think to look for you, right?" When Zania nodded, I had a scathingly brilliant idea. "Do you like liver?"

"You really are nuts, you know that?" Zania said then turned to Abigail and Kat, "She's completely crazy."

"No, she's not," said Abigail. "She's offering to help you. And I think you should at least think about it."

"Okay, but what's it got to do with liver?"

"I've got the perfect place for you hide and it comes with three meals a day. You may have to pretend you like liver, but we'll worry about that later. Come on, grab your stuff."

"Where am I going?" asked Zania. This was my first inkling that Zania was softening, but she stayed rooted to the spot.

"My grandmother owns a restaurant and she

lives above it. She's got a spare bedroom and I guarantee she won't ask any questions. Well, actually she'll ask a ton of questions, but we'll just make something up. We'll tell her you're having problems at home and stuff like that. She'll buy it. She likes to help people."

I picked up my camera and Zania's sleeping bag. "*Andalay*," I commanded, sweeping the floor with the sleeping bag as I waltzed toward the door.

"Wait," called Zania, before I reached the door. "You might as well hear my story before we go."

Trying not to show too much enthusiasm, I returned, spreading the sleeping bag on the floor. We all sat down, sweeping debris out of the way. Zania sighed an enormous sigh and started her story.

Chapter 4

"It's my mother's boyfriend, Wayne."

"Oh my God," said Abigail, horrified. "Is he abusing you?"

"No."

We all exchanged relieved glances.

"My mother has this new boyfriend. I don't want you to the get wrong idea about my mother, right? She doesn't date much, and at first we both really liked this guy."

"Excuse me," I said politely, not wanting to disturb her flow. I needed some background. "I was just wondering, are your parents divorced?"

"No. My dad died when I was three."

"Oh. Sorry," I said, feeling embarrassed for asking.

"Car accident. I was really little."

"That's so awful," said Abigail while Kat murmured sympathetically. We needed to get the story back on track so I helped Zania along.

"So, your mom has this boyfriend …"

Zania picked up the thread. "That's right. She met Wayne at a singles' dance at our church. He seemed pretty safe. At least, that's what we thought and for a while, things were going great. He took her to the Caribbean for a holiday, which was really nice."

"Is that where you're from," I asked.

"No," said Zania. "I was born in New Brunswick. Like, do you actually assume all black people are from the islands, or something?

"No, I'm sorry, I was just trying to get to know more about you. Look, I won't interrupt again, okay? Go ahead."

"Thank you," said Zania, with a hint of sarcasm.

"So when did things start going wrong?" asked Abigail, gently guiding the conversation back on track.

"At first he was really nice, then he starting acting like the man of the house. My mom was doing his laundry, running errands, making most of his meals. Stuff like that."

"Does he live with you?"

"No, not officially, but he was around most of the time. And in the beginning my mom was pretty happy, but she works really hard and it was getting really tiring. When it was just the two of us, we'd do everything together. Like housework and stuff, but when Wayne was there, she didn't want me to have to wait on him, so she did it all herself."

"That sucks," said Kat. "I mean for your mom. And you."

"Anyway, that's not the problem. Like I said, at first he was really nice, then after they got back from vacation, he got really demanding and a couple of times he yelled at her and threatened her. I got the feeling that if she hadn't backed down and kissed his butt, he would have hurt her, or both of us. My mom isn't happy with the way things are going, but we're scared of what might happen if she breaks up with him. She's just waiting for the right time, you know? Anyway, on Monday, Mom told me that he'd asked her to drop a bag off at his gym on her way to work. Except that the gym was out of her way and it was going to make her late for work."

"Wait a minute," I said. "Sorry to interrupt again, but does this jerk have a job?"

"Sure," said Zania. "He works for a printing company in Scarborough."

"Are you sure?" I asked.

"Well, no," said Zania, "Like, I never followed him to work or anything, but he leaves to go to work every weekday."

"Okay, what happened with the gym bag?"

"So, Mom asked me to take it for her. I took the bag and grabbed the subway. I'd be late for class but so what? Anyway, so there I am, on the subway, which was really packed and I got to thinking, 'Why doesn't Wayne take his own stinkin' clothes to the gym?' I mean, he's got a car, and here I am going out of my way on the subway to deliver some smelly sneakers for this jerk. So, I decided to sneak a peek. Big mistake."

Zania paused to look around. She hunched down to look under the shelf, and retrieved a bottle of water that had rolled under. It was all I could do to restrain myself from grabbing Zania and shouting "What was in the bag?!" Instead, I held my tongue while Zania took a long drink.

"So, sure enough, there was a T-shirt on top of a pair of runners. Just like I expected. But wrapped up in the T-shirt and inside the runners were these little plastic bags. Well, without thinking I pulled one out for a closer look. I'm not stupid and I knew before I had it in my hand it was drugs, but I couldn't stop myself. I'd completely forgotten I was on the subway. So there I was, in a car full of people, holding up a bag of drugs for everybody to see."

I was actually speechless, as we all stared at Zania, spellbound.

"I jammed the little bag back into the big bag and dropped the thing on the floor. I was so shocked I didn't know what to do. At first, I was afraid somebody would call the cops on a cell phone, or stop the train, but once I calmed down, it looked like nobody had even noticed. So I kind of relaxed and tried to figure out what to do next. By this time, I only had one stop to go. I got ready to go and reached down to pick up the bag, and it was gone."

We gasped in unison. "Oh my God," I said, horrified, "What did you do?"

"What could I do?" replied Zania. "Call the police? Like say, 'Excuse me, somebody stole my bag of drugs, would you mind getting it back for me? My mom's boyfriend is going to be seriously pissed.'"

"You didn't see who took it?" asked Kat.

"I looked at every person on that car and nobody had it. I guess whoever took it got off at the stop before."

"They obviously saw you take the drugs out," I said. "Of course they'd get off at the next station and walk out. Were you near the doors?"

"Yeah, I was."

"So then what did you do?" said Abigail. "Did you come straight here?"

"No, I got off the train and headed back downtown to my mom's office. I had to tell her what happened, because Wayne would find out eventually that the bag never got there. I can tell you that was probably the worst conversation I've ever had with my mother. I mean, we were in deep crap. Mom wanted to go to the police right away, but it's not like we had proof that Wayne was dealing drugs."

"Why did you think he was dealing the drugs? Maybe they were his," I said.

"There were a lot of those little bags," replied Zania. "Mom said they would be worth an astronomical amount of money. I mean, it's not like he went around stoned all the time. We never even knew he used."

Zania continued her story. "So if we accused him and they didn't find anything, who knows what he'd do to us? I have no idea how much money those drugs were worth, but I bet it was plenty. In the end, we both went home and practically ripped the apartment to bits looking for more drugs. We didn't find anything. So Mom told me to go to school and not to come back until she was sure it was safe. I didn't want to do it but I didn't know what else to do. I brought some stuff from home and my sleeping bag and figured I'd find someplace to hide out. That's how I wound up here."

"When was that, again?" I asked.

"Two days ago."

"What happened when your mom told Wayne you lost the bag?"

"That's the problem. I called the apartment and there was no answer. I called her back at work and they said she was off sick. I kept calling and one time Wayne answered. I didn't say anything and he guessed it was me because he started yelling and said to get my butt back to the apartment if I didn't want my mother to get hurt."

Up to this point, Zania had been fairly calm, but now she started crying again. Abigail put her arm around Zania while I said, "Don't worry Zania. We'll figure something out. She'll be okay as long as Wayne can't find you."

"Yeah," sniffed Zania. "That's what I figured. Mom said to stay away until she could let me know it was safe. I'm going to keep calling until I can talk to her. In the meantime, I'm scared to death he'll hurt her anyway. I hope she didn't tell him where I went. I'm not sure he knows where I go to school."

"Zania," said Abigail, "Don't you have any other relatives who could help?"

"No," said Zania. "My mom's family is still in New Brunswick. And I don't have enough money to go there. Besides I don't want to leave without Mom." Zania broke down into fresh tears.

I looked at my watch. "It's 5:30. We'd better get out of here." Then I looked around at all the props littering the floor. "But first, we clean up."

We gathered the scattered items and replaced them on the shelves, even the broken bits. At least this was one mess we *could* clean up. As for Zania's mess? That was going to take a bit more imagination.

Chapter 5

By the time we reached the restaurant, I'd worked up a reasonable story to tell Mémère. Seniors crowded the restaurant and there was the usual hum of friendly conversation between tables.

"It's cute, but how come there's only old people here?" Zania asked, looking around.

"Would *you* eat at a restaurant called *The Liver Spot*?" I replied.

"No way. I guess only old people eat liver."

"Yeah, that's for sure. Maybe it's an acquired taste. By the time we're their age, we'll be panting for liver. We call these guys the "Three Squares." They come in every day for all three meals. See that guy over there with the red bow-tie? That's Mr. Plawicki. He's Mémère's boyfriend."

"He is not my boyfriend. He's my lawyer." Mémère's voice made us both jump. Standing behind us, hands on her ample hips, she looked at Zania with open curiosity. "D'Arcey, who is your friend?"

"Mémère, this is Zania," I said. "Zania, this is Mémère." Mémère put her hand out and Zania took it, awkwardly. It looked to me that Zania wasn't used to shaking hands so Mémère enclosed Zania's limp hand in both of hers and squeezed. "You look hungry, Zania. Do you like liver?"

I groaned on Zania's behalf. "She does that to everybody, Zania. Don't look so worried. There's lots of other things on the menu. Mémère makes the best thick-cut fries in the whole world. And fried chicken to die for."

"*Bon*. I'll get cooking," said Mémère, bustling off behind the counter. "You sit here, Zania," she said, pointing to the stools at the counter. Then she disappeared into the kitchen.

"Is your grandmother mental for liver or what?" asked Zania, as soon as Mémère was out of range.

"Kind of. My great-grandfather was a butcher and they ate a lot of the parts of animals you don't want to think about. Mémère says it's why she's never been sick a day in her life. But if you ask me, it would make me sick to eat some of that stuff. Look out, she's coming back."

"Does your mother know you're here?" she wondered, looking at me.

"Yes, Mémère."

Mémère set two places in front of us. "She has the night off and she comes here anyway. She must have something important to tell me."

"You are *so* smart, Mémère," I said, giving my grandmother a great big sincere smile.

50

"You are *so* full of baloney, I could fry you up and serve you for breakfast."

"Well, that's a lovely thought, Mémère, but that would deprive you of my precious services, not to mention my company, which I happen to know you cherish because my mother told me so."

"Enough, Mademoiselle Smarty Pants. What do you want?"

Zania had remained silent during our banter, looking somewhat anxiously from me to Mémère and back again. We take a little getting used to, I'll admit.

"Well," I started. "Zania has a problem and I thought maybe you could help us out for a couple of days."

"Do you need a job, young lady?" asked Mémère. "We can always find you something to do."

"No, Mémère, although she'd be happy to help out, wouldn't you, Zania?" Zania nodded silently. "Actually," I lowered my voice and glanced around the restaurant to indicate the delicacy of the situation. "Zania's mom has this nasty boyfriend." Zania shook her head, alarmed, unwittingly playing into my scenario. Mémère looked quickly at Zania and reached for her hand.

"*Ma fille,*" she said in her most soothing tone, "You don't have to say anything. I understand." Zania let Mémère hold her hand, while looking beseechingly at me. A bell rang behind Mémère. "D'Arcey, *viens avec moi.*"

I followed my grandmother into the kitchen. As

the swinging door closed, Mémère rounded on me. "Did that man hurt the girl? Did you call the police?"

"I don't think so, at least not yet," I let my words sink in. "You see, he's moving out this week and they don't have any other family here, so her mother was going to send Zania to a hotel in case there was trouble but hotels are really expensive and it's not the best place for a young girl to stay alone, so I thought maybe you'd let her stay here. Until it's safe, you know."

"*Oui*, I know. Poor little thing. I knew right away she was scared of something. I will call her *maman*, let her know her girl is safe with me."

"No, that's okay, we already called her," I turned to the door. As I swung it open, I stopped, turned back and let it hit me on the butt. "Mémère, you rock!" As I continued backing out the door, I added, in my most confidential tone, "I don't think you should ask Zania too many questions, 'cause she really doesn't like to talk about it."

When I came out of the kitchen, Zania was chatting shyly with a pair of ladies at a nearby table. "We're cool," I said.

"Oh my God, D'Arcey, you scared the crap out of me" Zania whispered, "I thought you were going to tell her everything."

"No, just enough to let her draw her own conclusions. She has a very vivid imagination."

"Must run in the family," said Zania.

"I'm going to grab our food and we'll go upstairs

and plan our next move." I peered into the kitchen. "It's up, wait here." I bounced off my stool and dashed around the counter. At the door I stopped and called out "Incoming!" before flinging the swinging door inward. I grabbed the loaded plates and reversed the process. "The carrots are just for colour," I explained to Zania. "You don't eat them."

I plopped the plates onto a tray and said "Follow me." I led Zania to the narrow hallway leading to the rear of the restaurant. Beyond the two doors of men's and ladies' washrooms, I turned sharply, mounting a steep flight of stairs. At the top, I made a sharp right turn into the tiny kitchen and set the tray on the tiny bistro table. Zania followed me, saying "Whoops!" when she nearly knocked me flying.

"I'll show you around," I said, squeezing past her out the doorway into the hall. "That door at the end is the bathroom. This is Mémère's bedroom." I pushed open the door next to the kitchen. As always, the room was as neat as could be, with the bed perfectly made. I shut the door. "And this is where you'll sleep," I said, leading Zania into the living room and pointing to the sofa bed. "It's pretty comfortable. I sleep here a lot."

"There's a lot of stuff in here," observed Zania.

"Yeah, when the sofa bed is open, you have to climb over that chair to get into bed. Come on, let's eat."

In the kitchen I set two places while Zania stood in the doorway watching. With a grand flourish, I pulled a chair out for her and announced, "Dinner is served." Zania wasted no time plowing into her supper. The girl was obviously hungry after her recent diet of junk food. I let her eat quietly and slid the ketchup back and forth between us as we dunked our fries between murmurs of appreciation.

"I don't want to sound ungrateful," said Zania, "but really, why are you helping me? I mean, you never said a word to me since I started at school, so, what's up?"

Zania's question kind of floored me. Earlier she had been practically helpless, crying and moping and scared. Now *she* was grilling *me*! What was up with *that*? That girl had a suspicious streak a mile wide.

"'Cause you're in trouble, and that's what we Dufresnes do. We help people in trouble." No point in adding that this particular Dufresne was always on the lookout for a scoop.

Zania took a long time to respond, giving me a look that made me wonder if she could read minds. "Yeah, well, just try to remember that it's *my* problem, not yours."

Yeah, well, the way I saw it, it may have been her problem, but she wasn't in any position to solve it. But I was. And if it kick-started my career, so much the better. It's hard to get into university these days. There's probably a gazillion kids trying to get into journalism. It never hurts to have an ace up your sleeve.

"The way I see it," I said, waving a ketchup-coated French fry like a finger dipped in blood, "we've got to get a message to your mother and find out what Wayne's doing."

"I sent her an email but I didn't get a reply," said Zania. There she was reading my mind again. That was going to be my next question.

"Hmmm," I said, thinking. "Maybe Wayne intercepted it. What did you say?"

"Nothing much, just that I was okay and that I wanted to know how she was doing."

"Okay, I have an idea. I'm going over to your place. I'm going to go inside and start knocking on doors on your floor. I'll take the video camera and say I'm doing a documentary then I'll ask a bunch of questions. I'll work my way around the floor and try to get myself invited into your place."

At this, Zania became alarmed. "You can't go there alone. What if Wayne's there? It'd be way too dangerous."

"Why would it be dangerous? He doesn't even know me. "

"I just don't want you to say anything that'll make more trouble. What if he follows you here?" Zania remained agitated. I needed to reassure her.

"Right. I'll take Abigail, she can hold the camera while I do the interviews. Safety in numbers. And I promise I won't say anything that could possibly get your mother, or you, hurt."

Once again, Zania went from agitated to downright skeptical. I started wondering if there was someplace I could go to practise screaming. Just in case I needed to. There really isn't anywhere you do that, you know. Without drawing the wrong kind of attention. Like, how can you be sure you can get off a good scream when you need one?

"I have an idea," I said. "Let's try phoning your place and see who answers."

I charged out of the kitchen, returning moments later with Mémère's cordless phone. "Look at this antenna," I said, "I bet you can pick up signals from Mars or Venus. It's huge. Doesn't this phone look like something out of the seventies? Maybe even the fifties."

"I don't think they had cordless phones in the fifties," said Zania.

"I know that. But if they did, it would look like this." I handed the phone to Zania. "Just dial your number. I'll talk." As Zania punched the number out on the squishy keys, I had another thought. "What's your mother's name?"

"Rhonda," she said, then quickly thrust the phone at me as it began to ring at the other end.

The ringing went on forever, so I rolled my eyes and my head, miming boredom. When the woman's voice on the other end said "Hello?" I'd instantly forgotten who we were calling. The voice repeated, "Hello?" I blanked on the name Zania had just given me. "Oh, sorry. Is Zania there?" I stuttered, making a face at Zania.

"No, I'm sorry she's not home."

I wished I had a speaker phone so I could confirm that I was hearing Zania's mom's voice. I leaned down to let Zania listen but the connection was broken with no further comment from the woman.

"I don't know if that was your mom or not," I said to Zania. "She just said you weren't home." The phone in my hand rang, shocking me so that I dropped the phone. We both stared at it lying on the floor with the green lighted buttons pulsing with each ring. I snatched it up and said a cautious "Hello."

"Did you just call here looking for Zania Thomas?" My heart began to pound and I felt my face redden as though I had been caught doing something I shouldn't have done. Zania looked at me with alarm. The voice went on, "I said, are you looking for Zania?" Carefully, I put my hand over the mouthpiece and whispered, "I think it's Wayne!"

Zania gasped out loud. "Shhh!" I admonished, using the extra seconds to compose myself.

In a choked voice, I said into the phone "Um, yeah, I was just calling to, um, see how she's doing."

"She's not here. Who's calling?"

I needed time to think how to answer Wayne, but each second stretched out too long and I didn't want to raise his suspicions. When I finally decided what to say, I answered as nonchalantly as I could. "I used to go school with Zania before she transferred. That's why I was calling. I hadn't heard from her in a while and I just wanted to stay in touch. You know? Anyway, I gotta go." I was anxious to end the call, but Wayne was still talking at the other end.

"I asked you, who's calling," he said, his voice rising in volume.

What a rude jerk, I thought, searching for a name to give him. "Iona," I said. "Iona Kenmore. Thanks, 'bye!"

I clicked off the phone and pulled the batteries out. "Whew!"

"Iona Kenmore?" said Zania. "Who's Iona Kenmore?"

"Nobody," I said. "It's the toaster and refrigerator." I pointed to the toaster on the counter with the name "IONA" printed on the side, then to the nameplate on the refrigerator.

Zania laughed nervously. "Quick thinking."

"Not quick enough," I replied. "Do you have call display?"

"No," said Zania. "Oh yeah, then how did he get this number?"

"Call back feature, I guess. I gotta be more careful. If you had call display he'd have this number AND Mémère's name."

"What if he calls back when Mémère's here? What if Mémère asks me to answer the phone?"

"Mémère would never give her name or number to a stranger on the phone. And he's not going to ask for you. There's no reason on earth why he would think that you were here." It was only logical, but Zania was too freaked out to realize it herself. "I'll make sure Mémère knows that nobody is supposed to know you're here. She'll be cool. Hey, at least we know your mom's okay. Right? She sounded okay on the phone. Now we just have to figure out how to get her away from Wayne."

Chapter 6

After that near-disastrous phone call, I needed to really think our next steps through. Leaving Zania with Mémère, I gave her directions to my house and told her to meet me there after breakfast the next day. Then I conferenced Kat and Abigail and filled them in on events. The next day was Saturday and we had a whole day to work out a plan and act on it. I went to bed that night with a zillion scenarios in my head. By the time I drifted off, I had the beginnings of a workable operation.

I had just finished my breakfast and was scanning the front section of the newspaper when the doorbell rang. Rooter shot out of the kitchen, barking wildly and sliding on the tile floor. I knew it had to be Zania because around our house, only strangers ring the bell. My friends just open the door and yell "Halloooo!" Rooter still runs to the front door, but at least he doesn't bark.

"Hi Zania," I said, "Come on in." Leading her

into the dining room where my mother sat with a coffee and her own paper, I said, "Mom, this is Zania. She's working on my docudrama with us. Zania, this is my mom, Selena."

"Hello, Zania. I'm pleased to meet you."

"Hello," said Zania, rather shyly. "Mrs. Dufresne." Once we were inside my room, with the door closed, she looked around, saying, "Your mom seems nice."

"Yeah," I said. "Your mom sounds nice too." We just stood there, awkwardly, for a minute. "Hey, how was your night at Mémère's? You sleep okay on the sofa bed?"

"Yeah, it was okay. Mémère went to bed real early so I just watched TV until I was tired." She wandered around the room, looking at stuff and picking things up off my desk. "Hey, do you think I could borrow some clean clothes?"

"Sure," I said. Downstairs, the front door opened. "My closet is your closet. Pick anything you like." I ran out into the hall to meet Abigail and Kat. "Hi. Zania's already here," I said.

When we joined Zania in my bedroom, she stood in front of the open closet, kind of zoned out. "Zania needs some clean clothes to wear," I said.

"Oh, let me help," said Abigail, the fashionista, who then proceeded to load Zania up with half the contents of my closet.

"Can we get down to business, silver plate?" I asked.

"Silver what?" said Zania.

"Silver plate. It's French for 'please.'"

"It is not."

"It's the northern Ontario French-Canadian pronunciation."

Zania looked at Abigail, who shook her head. I ignored them both.

"I have an absolutely brilliant idea," I said.

Zania opened her mouth as if she was going to say something then shut it again. The other two remained mute on the bed.

"We're going to Zania's apartment in disguise as documentary film-makers."

"Why don't we just go pretend that we're taking pledges for a charity walk or something?" asked Kat.

Kat loves doing charity walks. She always thinks she's going to meet lots of boys. Then all she meets is a lot of other girls hoping to meet boys. "Because, Kat," I said, with more patience than I felt, "people don't like to give money to charity. But everybody wants to be a star!"

"Yeah but documentaries are boring. Nobody watches them."

"Yeah but you don't have to pay people to be in documentaries, Kat."

"Okay, okay!" interrupted Zania. "Can we just talk about what we're going to do when we go in there?"

"Well, first of all, you're not going anywhere because it's too dangerous. What if Wayne sees you?"

"Yeah, right. I didn't think of that."

"So, we disguise ourselves a bit, go in, knock on a couple doors on your floor, just to set the scene, then we see if we can get your mother to answer the door."

"What if Wayne's there?" Abigail asked.

I looked at Zania. "Is he usually there on the weekend?"

"Yes and no," she said. "I mean, I told you he doesn't actually live with us, so he kind of comes and goes."

"Look," I said, "I've thought about this a lot. If he's holding your mom prisoner, then he's probably gonna be there. If he's not, we're gonna ask her to come home with us. The problem is, from what Zania's told us, her mother doesn't think she has anywhere to go in Toronto that's safe. And she won't go anywhere without Zania anyway. We can take her to Zania and then, well, I haven't thought that far ahead." I paused. "But I will," I added.

Zania had her head in her hands at this point and her voice was low, coming through her fingers. "And if he's there, then what? Nothing."

"No," I hastened to reassure her. "I'll find a way to slip a message to your mother."

"Maybe we should wait until Monday, when Wayne's at work," Abigail suggested.

"No!" Zania and I said, loudly and in unison. "We have to do something, right now," I said, while Zania nodded her head in agreement. "We'll go back on Monday if we have to, but we've got to at least try now, while we have a chance."

"Okay," said Abigail. "What do I do?"

"Great," I said. "A.B., you're coming into the building with me. You'll handle the camera. Kat, you're outside, and Zania, you wait in the coffee shop with a cell phone."

"But I'm the cinematographer!" Kat blurted, her voice wavering.

"I know, I know," I soothed, "but we need somebody to watch the front of the building and the windows, Kat. And you're much better at that than A.B. and me."

"Like what? I'm good at just standing around looking at stuff and you're not?"

"No, no, no. You're good at observing and we're not. You notice things we don't." Which was not strictly true. Kat's attention tended to wander.

"Besides," added Abigail, "I'm not really videoing anything. I'm just there to help with the cover. Right?"

A thought occurred to me: we needed another prop.

"Yeah, right," I said, "We're only pretending to make a documentary. The only time we'll turn on the camera will be at Zania's apartment. You know what? I just thought of something. We need to get another camera for you. We really need a camera on the building."

"Do I still get to wear a disguise?"

"Absolutely," I said. "Let's grab some stuff out of the costume trunk." I have this great trunk full of old clothes, hats, wigs and stuff that I collected over the years. Most of it is from Mom and Mémère, but I got lots of things from the thrift stores. Anything that looked vintage, like from the sixties and seventies.

Kat grabbed a short, brown curly wig and pulled it on her head. She stuffed her long thick hair under the cap, struggling to hide all of it. Instantly, she looked a few years older.

"We need hats," I said. "So the wigs won't look so fake. Mom has a bunch of berets. That'll make us look arty. Like documentary film-makers."

"What do documentary film-makers wear?" asked Kat.

"Black. I think they wear black. Loose black clothes and no make-up. And glasses, we'll all need glasses."

"But won't we all look alike?" asked Abigail.

"Exactly alike. Which is perfect because nobody will be able to distinguish us from each other. We'll be clones."

"Cool," said Kat. "Like goths."

"Yes," I said. "Let's be gothic film-makers. We need black wigs. Longer would be better, but we can't be picky."

"Wait a minute," interrupted Abigail. "If we look like goths people won't want to talk to us."

"Right," I said. "We'll be friendly goths. Make that brown wigs."

Abigail found a reddish-brown shoulder-length wig and, with Kat, pored through my costume trunk. Most of clothes in the trunk were far too colourful for surveillance. Kat extracted a shimmering red beaded bra. "Look at this," she said to Zania. "This is from when D'Arcey wanted to be a belly-dancer."

"Yeah," said Abigail. "And her mom wouldn't let her out of the house in that thing. She wore it over a T-shirt on Hallowe'en. Her dad followed us all over the neighbourhood to make sure she didn't take the T-shirt off."

I didn't have enough dark clothes so I raided my mom's wardrobe. While I was in there, I found our old video camera. It used VHS tapes so it was at least three times as big as our new digital one.

"It's so big!" protested Kat. "I'm going to get a cramp."

"Don't worry," I said. "You get the small one. This was my dad's first camcorder. It's vintage, almost fifteen years old. We're going to dress it up like a news camera. While I make our ID, look for a shoulder bag that you can cut a hole in for the camera lens."

On my computer, I launched a graphics program and printed some new DNN stickers to put on the camera. From my desk drawer, I pulled out three plastic name-tag holders on strings. Into these, I put my official DNN press passes with fake names. Once we were all dressed and wearing our near-identical berets, I handed out the identification.

"Put those under your sweaters until we need them," I said. "But memorize your names. We can't use our real names. Ever. It could be fatal."

"Janet Jackson. That's imaginative," complained Kat.

"I'm Janine Lavigne," said Abigail.

"Yes, and I'm Janice Osborne," I replied. "We all have similar first names. It's easy for us to remember and confusing for anybody else. Now let's get going. I'd better check in with Selena. You guys just keep going down the stairs and out the side door."

As we tromped down the stairs, we could hear my mom humming. Then, I stepped into the dining room where my mother was marking papers at the table. "That's quite an outfit," she said.

"I'm going out for a while to work on my docu-drama."

"All right D'Arcey. Don't be late at the restaurant."

"I won't. I'll go straight there." I was pretty much out the door by the time I finished talking.

"Are we gonna walk or take the streetcar?" Kat asked.

"I dunno," I said. "Everybody got their passes?" We decided to take the TTC. At Bathurst and St. Clair we stopped with Zania in front of the coffee-shop on the corner.

"That's it over there. The yellow brick one," Zania pointed north to a highrise building. "My apartment's on the other side. Facing east. Fourth floor."

"Okay," I said. "You go inside and have a coffee or something and wait for us to call. Have you got my phone?"

"Yeah," she replied, holding it up.

"You got your phone?" I asked Abigail. She held hers up. "*Andalay.*" I led the way.

Zania's building was off Bathurst Street among new retirement condos. Lots of older people walked to and from St. Clair this morning. As we approached, I scanned the street to find a good spot for Kat to sit and observe the building. A park on the east side of the building busted with dogs and their walkers. With its benches and trees, it was perfect spot for Kat to wait.

Kat used the time on the TTC to practise filming with the camera inside the bag. It wasn't easy but by the time we arrived at the park, she said she was confident she could get some good footage. The bench she chose gave a reasonably good side view of the entrance to the building as well as Zania's fourth floor windows.

"Look," I said, "There's the blue curtains and the plants just like Zania said."

"Oh, I see it," said Kat, lifting her arm. I grabbed it and said urgently, "Don't point!" Then I added, "Don't look, just scan the area, like you're bored or something. Come on, A.B., we've got work to do."

"How long will you be gone?" asked Kat, glancing around nervously.

"Not too long," I said. "There are ten apartments on the floor but we're only going to hit two or three before we go to Zania's, just to make it look random. We won't spend more than five minutes with each. Like I said, if we find Zania's mom alone, we'll try to bring her out with us."

We left Kat on the bench, adjusting her bag to aim the lens. I had put a purple rubber key identifier on Zania's front door key. We entered the building and went directly to the elevator. As we waited, I scoped the lobby and checked for additional exits. A side exit faced the park. I chided myself for not noticing the door when we were on that side of the building. When the elevator arrived, I rushed forward, straight into a man trying to exit. We bumped and my wig shifted slightly. I had to clutch my head to keep the wig from slipping further. The man looked at me curiously and then at Abigail, who stood aside to let him pass with a completely blank look on her face. And then, without a backward glance, the man hurried out of the building. By the time the elevator doors closed he was gone.

"This wig is too big. I should have pinned it on." I tugged at the wig, which only made it skew worse. Abigail put her bag down and straightened my hair seconds before the elevator pinged to announce our arrival on the fourth floor.

I slipped the DNN badge out of my sweater. Abigail did the same, then pulled my microphone out of the bag. "Do you have any idea what you're going to say?" she asked, handing me the mic.

"It depends on who opens the door," I replied. "We just have to get them to talk to us for a couple of minutes. Well, here goes." Rather anticlimactically, our first few knocks got no response. When we finally reached an apartment with someone at home, I was ready with my pitch.

The middle-aged woman who opened the door looked with mildly puzzled amusement at us.

"Hello, my name is Janice Osborne. We're documentary film-makers. Do you have a few minutes to be interviewed?"

The woman's smile broadened and she said, "Sure." She started to pose when Abigail raised the video camera and trained it on her. "What's your documentary about?" she asked.

"It's about multiculturalism in Toronto," I said, lifting the microphone to my mouth and asking the woman her name. Quickly, I shoved the microphone in the woman's face.

"Karen," she said, still smiling.

I pulled back my microphone and turned to Abigail with the camera. "Karen, how long have you lived in Toronto?" I asked. Immediately, I whipped around again and pointed the microphone at Karen, who was now laughing. Abigail played along, following the exchange with her camera.

"I came to Toronto in the early eighties," she said. "From Montreal."

"Would you tell us why you came to Toronto?" I intoned into the mic.

Karen leaned into the microphone, smiled at the camera and said cheerfully, "Because all my friends were moving here and I didn't want to be lonely in Montreal."

By this time, I realized that I didn't have a plan

on how to wrap up the interview and Karen looked quite comfortable leaning on the door chatting with us. This could take longer than I'd planned.

"Karen, you've been in Toronto a long time. Do you ever wish you had never left Montreal?"

"Sometimes. But not enough to go back," she said.

"So, you'd say you like living in Toronto?"

"Yes, I'd say that," said Karen.

"Thank you, Karen," I said, looking into the camera again. "Cut."

"So, will I see your documentary on TV or something?" asked Karen.

"Oh, maybe," I said, nonchalantly. "Thanks, we have to go now. We need to get a lot more interviews done today."

We walked down the hall, waving furiously at Karen, hoping she would go inside and close her door. I kept pushing Abigail along until we made it around the corner out of Karen's sight.

"Yipes," I whispered. "I had no idea it was going to be that hard to get away. I was afraid to knock on the next door in case Karen just hung out and started a big block party."

"Yeah, well now what do we do?" asked Abigail. "I thought we needed to establish our cover."

"You know what?" I said, "We'll just do one more, so Karen doesn't get suspicious and then we'll go see if there's anybody home at Zania's."

We peeked cautiously around the corner to see if Karen was still lurking in her doorway but she was gone and her door was closed. Zania's apartment was near the elevator, so I chose one as far from either Zania's or Karen's as we could get. My knock brought an elderly man to the door. This apartment occupant was a great deal more suspicious than Karen. He eyed us with a sour look as I said, "Good afternoon, sir. We're documentary film-makers ..."

"No, no. No, no, no," he muttered, quickly shutting the door on us.

"I think that went well," I said. "I have an idea. Come here," I led Abigail back to the first door we had knocked on. Rapping on the door, I waited a few seconds before announcing loudly to the empty corridor, "Hello, we're documentary film-makers. May we ask you a few questions?" After a short pause, I put my hand over my mouth and said, "Waa, waa, waa."

"Thank you," I went on, "How long have you lived in Toronto?" Abigail, catching on said, in an unnaturally high voice, "Fifty years."

"Wow," I said. "Were you born here?"

"No," said Abigail, "I was born in Edmonton."

"That's really nice," I said. "Thank you. We'll be in touch. Buh bye."

Giggling, we scampered back around to the other side of the building. Time for the most important interview of the day. I drew in a big breath and rapped on Zania's door. The sound hung in the air so I pressed my ear to the door, to listen for movement inside. "It's quiet," I said. "No wait, I think I hear something!" I stepped back from the door, but still no one answered. "I'm going to knock again. I think there's someone in there," I said. Knocking again, I announced myself as a documentary film-maker in case Zania's mom was afraid to open the door to strangers.

Still there was no answer. "I'm sure I heard something," I insisted.

"What are we going to do?" said Abigail.

"I was prepared for this." I pulled a small envelope out of my pocket and slipped it under the door.

"What is that?" said Abigail.

"Sshh." I pulled Abigail away from the apartment door and led to her to the elevators. Still whispering, I said, "It's a note to tell her to call the cellphone."

"What cellphone?" said Abigail.

"Mine. The one Zania has."

The elevator pinged and once again I lurched into the car and straight into the same blond guy I'd bumped into earlier.

"Hey," he said, "Watch it."

"Sorry,"

"You with some kinda cult?"

The elevator doors closed on me saying "We're documentary film-makers."

Kat leaped off the park bench and ran to meet us. "Did you see her? Was she there?"

"Nah," I said. "I mean, I think she was in there, but she didn't answer the door."

"D'Arcey left her a message."

"Let's get back to Zania."

"I thought you were supposed to call her," said Kat.

"It's only half a block. I'll tell her that we struck out when we see her. Let's go." Actually, I was stalling. I didn't want to have to tell Zania we'd failed in this attempt.

We walked briskly back to the coffee shop where Zania was sitting with an empty cup and the cellphone in front of her. Her disappointment was obvious from the second she saw us enter without her mother.

"No go," I said. "But I think she was in there." We all jumped when the phone rang. I stared at it dumbly, momentarily confused about why someone was calling. After all, it wasn't technically my phone. It was my brother's. He had very conveniently forgotten it the last time he was home.

"Pick it up!" urged Zania.

Flipping open the cover I said, "Hello?" Static interfered with the reception and I could barely hear the caller. "Hello?" I repeated. The noise on the line cleared enough for me to hear the caller say "Zania" but I was still unsure whether the caller was a man or a woman.

"Rhonda?" I asked, tentatively. The other three girls tensed.

"Is that you Zania?" The voice came through clearly enough for me to know it was a man on the other end.

Boldly, I retorted, "No it's not. Where's Rhonda?"

"Never mind Rhonda. I know you called her last night. You tell Zania to get her butt over here before there's any more trouble."

"I'd be happy to do that, sir," I said, "but first I have a message for Rhonda. May I speak to her please?" Although my voice was calm, I was sweating buckets.

The man shouted an obscenity into the phone. In the background, I honestly believed I could hear a noise like a woman crying or pleading. The signal was fading again.

"I can't tell you where Zania is until I talk to Rhonda," I shouted into the phone, drawing annoyed stares from the coffee-shop's staff and customers. "I have to talk to Rhonda!"

"!@#$#%!" That came through loud and clear but nothing further came from the witless jerk on the other end. I wasn't certain that Wayne was still on the line.

"You tell Zania to get over here with my property or her mother is dead."

"I beg your pardon?" I had heard Wayne perfectly well, but that was the best retort I could come up with at that moment.

"You heard me."

Chapter 7

Well, there it was. An actual threat. I was the only one who'd heard it. Should I tell Zania? I didn't want her to do anything rash, like maybe try to save her mother by herself.

Zania shook me out of my reverie. "What happened?"

I looked at her and made my decision. "That was Wayne. He's an idiot, you know. He has a very limited vocabulary. He just wanted to know where you were." I turned off the cellphone and slid it into my pocket, wondering for a moment what Derek's outgoing message said, in case Wayne called back.

"We should call the police," said Abigail.

"And tell them what?" I replied, exasperated. "Look, I've got to go to the restaurant now. We can talk later."

"What do you want us to do with the cameras and stuff?" asked Kat.

"Oh yeah, can you drop them at my house for me?" I said.

"Don't you want to go over the video with Zania?"

"Nah. There's nothing on there. You said there wasn't anybody at the window. I'll look at it later when I get home. Talk to you later."

Zania and I walked back to the restaurant in near silence. She was obviously disappointed. We arrived at *The Liver Spot* and I looked around for Mémère, catching a glimpse of her through the kitchen window. Leaving Zania to set tables, I entered the kitchen to announce our arrival to my grandmother.

"Who are you?" asked Mémère.

"I'm D'Arcey," I said, thinking maybe Mémère had somehow slipped into senility since breakfast.

"No, I mean, who are you *today*?" Mémère removed my beret and straightened the wig. "Are you that reporter on TV?

"Yes," I said, pleased that Mémère had made the connection. "I'm working on my docudrama about Great-uncle Hubert."

"Bah, Hubert," said Mémère with disdain. "He was so vain, he wouldn't wear his glasses. Who drives a boat at night without glasses? A fool."

"How do you know he wasn't wearing his glasses?"

"Because I have them upstairs. They work pretty good for crosswords."

I sniffed around the kitchen a bit, looking in

pots for fries.

"Zania is pretty good at crosswords too," said Mémère, watching me.

"She is?"

"Yes, she is a very smart girl."

"She is?" I used a long fork to spear a fry in the hot oil.

"If she's your friend, you should know that already."

"She's a *new* friend, Mémère. She just started at my school."

"Then you should be spending more time to get to know her."

And I was going to get right on that, just as soon as I made sure she wasn't going to get killed by that maniac, Wayne.

I went back into the dining room to find Zania. "Listen," I said. "I have an idea. When we're finished we'll go out and look for a payphone. That way, if Wayne's at your place, he can't call us back."

Zania nodded in agreement, following me back to the tables. It was going to be a long lunch hour.

* * *

By the time the last customer left, and we had cleared the tables and loaded the dishwasher, Zania was so wired she was spinning like a top. She shot out of the restaurant dashing up the street, leaving me in the dust.

"Hey, wait up!" I chugged along at my fastest walking rate and finally caught up with her. Zania ducked into a convenience store in search of a payphone — a near-futile effort. Through the window of a sports bar, I spied one on a back wall, but when we entered, the owner turned us away because we were underage. Discouraged, we trudged all the way to the subway where we were pretty certain to find a phone on the platform. Although we were dangerously close to Zania's building, we had to risk it.

Before we reached the bottom of the steps, Zania started sprinting. She grabbed the receiver in her hand but had to wait for me because she didn't have a quarter. She'd left all her tips at the restaurant.

"Wait," I said. "Do you know what you're going to say?"

"No, and I don't care. I just want to hear her voice and find out if she's all right."

I watched her dial the phone, absolutely certain that Wayne would answer. To my complete surprise, Zania shouted "Mom!" and burst into tears. Maybe Wayne wasn't there. My mind began to race. We were so close to the apartment. Maybe we could run over and rescue Zania's mom!

That fantasy quickly exploded when Zania's expression turned from one of joy to extreme agitation. Wayne was there. I just knew it. Now Zania was nodding and saying "Uh huh" dully. I could barely restrain my hand from reaching out to snatch the phone. It was a mercifully short conversation, ending in renewed tears.

"What! For heaven's sake, Zania, what did she say?" I hated seeing Zania's tear-streaked face. Passerbys shot us some curious looks, so I led Zania up the stairs into the cool evening. "Come on," I said, "Let's go to the coffee shop."

The short walk felt interminably far because I had to drag Zania the whole way. While we waited for our lattes, Zania went to the washroom to wipe her face. When she re-emerged, she looked only slightly more composed.

"She wants me to come home."

"Are you crazy?! He's still there, isn't he?"

"Yeah." Zania fiddled with her cup, turning the handle from side to side.

"You can't go back. Zania, are you listening to me? It's a trap."

The noise in the busy coffee-shop almost drowned out Zania's reply. "Mom says it's okay."

"It's a lie!" My voice rose to a shout.

"My mother doesn't lie to me!" Zania shouted back.

Again, people stared at us — some annoyed and others frankly curious. "I know she wouldn't lie to you, Zania," I said, "but Wayne was standing right there and she couldn't say anything else. Think about it for a minute." Then I told Zania about Wayne's threat.

"Why didn't you tell me that before?" cried Zania. I looked around, and said "Shhh. Zania, we'll get your mother out of the apartment. We've got all day tomorrow. I promise."

"I can't take any more of this!" moaned Zania.

"Don't worry," I said in my most reassuring voice. "You can count on me."

Chapter 8

The truth was, I didn't have a clue how to extract Zania's mother from Wayne's clutches. Completely exhausted from the excitement and intensity of the day, I fell quickly into a deep sleep. I'm not an early riser and, truthfully, I'm just the tiniest bit dull in the morning, but I awoke feeling quite a lot more confident about finding a solution to Zania's nightmare. A long, refreshing shower provided me with enough concentrated thinking time to come up with a workable plan.

Now, I would gather my troops and march on the apartment building. But my first order of business was to eat an enormous breakfast. The sweet, sweet smell of maple sausages compelled me down the stairs into the kitchen.

"D'Arcey! Honey, you're late. Didn't you hear me calling you?" My mother slammed an enormous pancake onto a plate. Two, and then three sausages joined it. She placed the plate in front of me. I poured syrup instead of answering my mother.

"We have to leave in fifteen minutes," Mom said.

"Yeah, so," I mumbled through a mouthful of pancake. "I'm okay. I'll clean up."

"No, D'Arcey, *you* have to leave. We all have to leave. Don't you remember? We're going to Waterloo for Derek's game?"

"Oh, sh--" I gulped.

"D'Arcey!!"

"Shoot. Oh shoot. I can't go, Mom," I said, mental wheels grinding out a plausible excuse. "I've got so much homework. You won't believe it."

"Well, I would believe it, dear. I'm a teacher and we like to give homework. Except you told me you had it all done on Friday night."

Yikes — the dreaded parent who actually listened. Homework was a pretty lame excuse at any rate. I found it incredibly difficult to lie effectively when under the spell of maple-cured sausage. I wondered what my mother would do if I were to say, "Gee Mom, sorry, but I've got to go save an innocent woman from a fiendish drug dealer. You know how it is. Don't hold dinner for me."

Truth to tell, I was actually looking forward to going to Derek's university football game. I was reasonably certain an unbelievable number of really good-looking college jocks would attend and I promised to take acres of video to share with Kat.

I said a silent prayer that Zania's mother would be safe for another day and ran upstairs with

Derek's cellphone to call Zania at Mémère's.

It was incredibly hard to break the news to her.

"Why didn't tell me this yesterday? I thought you said we had all day today," said Zania accusingly.

"I forgot." I said, telling the lame truth. "Listen," I added, "why don't you come with us?" I was worried that Zania would get herself into trouble if I couldn't keep tabs on her.

"No, I think I'll just stay here with your grandmother. She's teaching me how to bake. I've never done that before."

"Okay," I said. "I'll call you if we get back early enough."

I was still worried about what Zania might do, so I made a fast call to Abigail.

"A.B.," I said, "*Ç'est moi*. Look, I need you to drop by the restaurant and take Zania somewhere. I don't care, as long as it isn't back to her apartment. Keep her busy." And then I explained what was going on. Abigail promised to keep Zania out of trouble until I got back. I clicked off and ran to the car where my parents were waiting.

It took a long time for my guilt to wear off. During the drive, I honed my plan for Monday, but once the game started, I threw myself into cheering for the home team. We got back way too late to call Zania or Abigail, so I sent a text message to A.B. hoping she'd get back to me before I met up with Zania in the morning.

On Monday morning I packed my disguise and video camera along with my school gear. Needing to confirm some details for the plan, I left early for the restaurant to meet Zania. When I went upstairs to get her, her appearance shocked me.

"Holy crap, Zania," I said, "You look like a zombie. Are you all right?"

"No. I am not all right. My mother's boyfriend is going to kill her if I don't go home so what am I doing instead? I'm sleeping on a sofa bed over a restaurant. I was this close to sneaking out last night and going home. Meanwhile, the great detective is off watching football."

"Hey," I said, annoyed at Zania's tone. That girl could be downright prickly. "I didn't have a choice, okay? And I honestly forgot. I said I was sorry. What more do you want?"

Zania put her head down on the kitchen table. "I want it to be over," she mumbled. "You have no idea what this is like. It's not a game. It's my life, and it sucks."

Did Zania really believe that I thought this was all just a game? I didn't. Really. More like a real-life drama. With a happy ending. And I, D'Arcey Dufresne, girl reporter-slash-righter-of-wrongs, was going to make sure of it.

"So, why didn't you sneak out?" I asked, grateful that she hadn't.

"Because your grandmother heard me get up. I

thought all old people were partially deaf."

"Nah. Only old men get deaf. Old ladies get bat hearing."

"Well, anyway, I didn't sleep after that."

"Yeah, obviously. Well, look, we're gonna get your mom out of the apartment today and then you can probably both stay at Mémère's until the police get Wayne."

"If they believe us."

"Don't worry, they will. We're gonna call him and record him making threats. That should be enough."

Zania thought for a while. "How are you gonna get Mom out of the apartment if he's there?"

I needed clarification on that detail. "You said Wayne works, right?" Zania nodded. "He wouldn't miss work, so he won't be at the apartment. I'm going to just open the door with your key and walk right in. Grab your mother. Walk out. Grab a cab. Hide at Mémère's. Call the police. Wayne goes to jail. You go home. Bada bing, bada bang, bada boom."

"If it's that easy, why didn't you just do that on Saturday?"

"Because Wayne doesn't work on Saturday," I said. "He might have been there. He *was* there!"

The sidewalk teemed with people hurrying to their destinations. Streetcar islands overflowed and a steady flow of commuters moved back and forth across the street heedless of the traffic signals. People walked with their heads down, paying no attention to other pedestrians and many times Zania and I split apart to avoid colliding with someone lost in their own thoughts. After one such encounter we came together again and I finally answered Zania's question.

"Zania, we couldn't just go in there without doing some recon, you know?" We waited for the light to change and were almost swept into the intersection by impatient pedestrians who couldn't wait for the signal. "We had to scope out the exits and time our escape. And we had to plan our route. Besides, we couldn't be sure if Wayne was really threatening your mom. But now we know everything we need to know and we're good to go."

"Today." It wasn't a question.

"Yes, Zania, today. We're going at lunch. You said Wayne works in Scarborough, so there's no way he can get from work to your house during his lunch hour. I've got it all figured out. No sweat. It's a classic surgical strike. A.B., Kat and I go to the apartment. We take the elevator to the fourth floor. Kat holds the elevator. A.B. and I go to your door. We open the door without knocking. We sweep the rooms. We grab your mom and do a dash for the elevator. We leave the building by the side door. We run into the apartment building across the street, the one with the doorman, and we ask him to call us a cab. Then we hightail it over to *The Liver Spot*. Stash your mother with Mémère. Back to school in time for Media Studies. Can't fail."

Zania stopped on the sidewalk while I walked

on a few more steps. When I looked back at her, her face turned stony and she said "If it doesn't work, I'm going back. I don't care. I can't leave her there alone."

I could understand that. In the meantime, I was absolutely certain that our plan was going to work, because, frankly, the alternative sucked.

"What time's your lunch period?" I asked.

"12:45."

"Good, we'll meet up in the cafeteria. We should be there by the end of your lunch." We parted company because our lockers and our first classes were in different parts of the school. "Don't worry," I called, as Zania walked away, her weariness evident in her heavy stride. "Everything's going to be okay."

* * *

I met up with Abigail at our lockers. "You got your stuff?" I asked.

"Yeah," Abigail replied, opening her pack to reveal the wig and the rest of her disguise. "I had to leave a couple of books behind."

"Okay, we meet here right after third period," I said. "We have five minutes to change and fifteen minutes to get over there by streetcar. I figure we need no more than fifteen minutes in the building. Five minutes to wait for the cab, ten minutes to Mémère's, ten minutes back to school. That's an hour. *Morçeau de gâteau.*"

"What if the streetcar's late?"

88

"We have fifteen minutes' slack."

"What if Wayne's there?" Kat voiced the main fear on my mind. But I'd convinced myself that Wayne couldn't possibly be there and I had to convince Abigail and Kat too.

"I'd call him at work, but Zania doesn't know the name of the company where he works. We looked in the phone book but she didn't recognize any of the names."

"That's not exactly reassuring," said Abigail, full of doubt.

"He goes to work every weekday. Zania was absolutely certain of that. It's Monday, so he's at work. Look A.B., I even asked her if he's a delivery guy or a salesman or anything that would mean he could leave work anytime he wanted. She said no. So we've gotta be safe."

"I keep wondering why her mom doesn't just walk out on her own. I mean, I'm pretty sure she could go to the police and they'd protect her, especially if he threatened her."

I thought about this for a second. "Because he has her tied up or something. That's why she doesn't answer the phone or the door when he isn't there."

No more time remained for speculation. It was time to act. As we walked into class I wondered if I was asking too much of my friends. I shouldn't have told them about Wayne's threat. I assumed all along that Kat and Abigail were as pumped as I was to be involved in this caper. I had been waiting all my life for this. I wasn't just pretend-reporting on a story, I was actually part of it. I'd save a woman from certain death and put a dangerous drug dealer behind bars. And I was only sixteen. I'd be featured on TV, maybe the national news would send a reporter. This was just the beginning.

"D'Arcey. D'Arcey Dufresne! Are you going to take your seat or stand guard at the door for the rest of the period?"

I hadn't realized I was standing just inside the classroom door. The class snickered like a bunch of twits. I strode majestically to my desk, slid elegantly into my seat and opened my textbook. English Literature is one of my best subjects. Consequently I feel a great moral superiority to those of my classmates who only endure the class because it's compulsory. I love the language and the stories, and if I hadn't already decided to be a television journalist, I'd probably be a great writer.

Unfortunately, once seated, I realized that I had to go to the bathroom. Usually, I make the trip to the bathroom immediately before class, but I'd been too busy working out the plan with Abigail and had missed my opportunity. Now I desperately needed to go. So, having only just sat down, I arose again and drifted back to the door, not unnoticed by our teacher.

"Are you expecting someone, D'Arcey? Or are you just making sure you're not late for your next class?" A less secure student might have found this comment and the attendant laughter embarrassing, but not I. I announced, in my most compelling television reporter voice, that I needed a commercial break.

I wasted no time in completing my business. The doors to both the boys' and girls' washrooms resided in a small alcove, which was probably one of the biggest design flaws in the history of high school architecture. Students collided and complained during high-traffic periods. At this moment, no traffic crowded me and I barrelled, unobstructed, back into the hallway. I shot out of the alcove into the centre of the corridor, scraping past someone moving purposefully in the opposite direction. The near-miss caused us to turn and look at each other.

What I saw in that split second caused me to stumble and very nearly fall flat on my face. Only my will to keep composure made me move without looking back to make sure of what I'd just seen. I wanted to, but really, I had no doubt. And the man, in that split second in which our eyes met, appeared slightly puzzled. But there wasn't any time to waste. I had to find Zania. Now.

It's a big school and I couldn't remember where Zania's first class was. But at least I knew my way around. On my way past my locker, I stopped to grab my pack. Thankfully, I had left everything in the locker and only taken my textbook and notes into class. "Think," I said under my breath, spinning the combo lock in a well-rehearsed pattern. "I have English first period, that's what I told her and she said … what? What did she say she had? Come on, D'Arcey. She said something. Like Chemistry? No, History!

That's it." Relieved, both by my recollection and the lock snapping open in my hand, I snatched my pack, locked the locker and ran down the hall.

I passed a couple of people, teachers maybe, but kept up my pace until I huffed up to the room. There was a small window in the door, but I didn't waste any time scoping the classroom through it. I simply burst through the door and without a pause announced, "Zania Thomas is wanted in the principal's office. Family emergency." The History teacher stared in surprise at the unexpected intrusion, but before he could even phrase a comment or raise an objection, Zania stood and followed me out the door.

"What's happened?' Zania cried.

"Sshhh!" I hissed back. "Just keep moving." I stopped abruptly at the intersection of two corridors. After taking a fast glance both ways we proceeded. Grabbing Zania by the arm, I hustled her out the doors into the bright sunlight.

"I don't have my coat!"

I managed to unzip part of my pack while running away from the school. "Here." I handed Zania the black tunic top I'd worn on Saturday. Zania struggled to pull on the top and still keep moving. We dashed westbound along St. Clair, taking frequent glances over our shoulders and many chances crossing the side streets against the lights.

"Where are we going?" Zania huffed and puffed while I alternately dragged and pushed her from behind.

"Here," I said, steering her into a large coffee-shop. The warmth might have been welcome after the chill outside, but we were both sweating from our mad dash. I selected a table at the back — one that couldn't be seen easily from the front window or the door.

"Stay here, I'll get coffee." Shortly after, I returned with a tray holding two cups of coffee and two crullers. Without touching either the coffee or my cruller, I picked up my pack and pulled out the video camera. In it was the tape that Kat had used on Saturday. Impatiently, I fast-forwarded the footage in the viewer, hoping that Kat had been on the ball that day. "Here he is," I said, and turned the camera to Zania. "Is that Wayne?"

Zania gasped as she watched the blond man from the elevator walk around the side of her apartment building and then disappear from view. "Yeah," she whispered, "That's him."

I felt confused, horrified and exhilarated — all at the same time. Why didn't I think of it before? The elevator man was Wayne. And Wayne stalked around the school at this very moment, looking for Zania.

"He's white," I said, dumbfounded. "I had no idea."

"You never asked," said Zania.

"Still, you might have said." My mental picture of the whole scenario was crumbling. I had imagined that Wayne was one of those sleazy druggie types on TV cop shows. And I had assumed that because Zania was black, Wayne was too.

"My mom's white too," said Zania.

"Oh." I picked up my cruller and munched pensively. "I guess you'd better tell me what she looks like."

Zania shot me a look and took quite a long time to answer. "Why didn't it matter what she looked like when you thought she was black?"

"Well," I said, thinking furiously. How was I going to say this without pissing Zania off? "Look, I just figured she looked like you so if we ran into her wandering around the building, I'd be able to recognize her. I mean, you didn't have a picture or anything we could look at, did you?"

"And now?"

I said, "And now, it doesn't matter anyway."

We were getting off track. The game had heated up dramatically and all my assumptions were flying out the window. I had assumed Wayne would be at work. He wasn't.

As if she could read minds, Zania said "Now what?"

But I only smiled thinly and drank my coffee.

—————

Chapter 9

My parents raised my brother and me to be self-reliant and self-confident. So maybe I was a little over-confident. But then again I wasn't afraid to learn something by trying, and I usually accepted the consequences of my choices. I'll admit, at first I'd gotten involved because it was a chance to break a big story. Along the way, I'd made some promises to Zania and I was as determined as ever to see the thing through to the end. While Zania's state of mind had swung from optimism to doubt and back, I pretty much knew I could get Zania out of this jam.

Except now I wasn't so sure. Until a few days ago, bad dudes like Wayne had shown up only on the nightly news. One thing I knew for certain, although I wasn't about to tell Zania. The cat and mouse game had gone on too long and Wayne wasn't going to wait forever for the mouse to go home. The time to end the game had come.

agged Zania to Mémère's, and told my
dmother that Zania was sick. After installing
ania upstairs and advising her to stay in the bathroom to avoid Mémère's certain curiosity, I went
back to school.

By that time, lunch was half over and Abigail
and Kat would be wondering what had become of
me. All the way back to school, I told myself that
Wayne hadn't recognized me — that Wayne
couldn't possibly have recognized me out of disguise and that certainly by now, someone would
have asked him to leave because he had no business being there. The school officials enforced
security strictly. Although Wayne might have spun
some story about Mrs. Thomas sending him to get
Zania. Well, Zania was safely out of his clutches
and soon, Zania's mom would be too.

Abigail and Kat sat in the cafeteria with some of
our other friends. When they saw me they launched
themselves across the room, *eliciting* curious looks
from the other girls. I walked back to the table with
them and when they asked where I had disappeared
to, I replied, "Cramps." As an all-purpose excuse,
it couldn't be beat, and if I had to duck out again, I
had established my alibi. I tried to eat my lunch
calmly as though nothing was wrong, deflecting
the probing looks of Abigail and the outright stare
of Kat.

As the various occupants of the table broke to
return to class, Abigail and Kat fell in step with
me, heading to the lockers.

"I saw Wayne."

"No way!" they exclaimed, genuinely surprised.

"He was here."

"Here? In school?" asked Abigail.

"Yeah. I grabbed Zania and took off."

"Wait a minute," said Kat "How did you know it was Wayne?"

I told them how I put two and two together and came up with Wayne. Then, I ran the tape again for Kat, who hadn't seen him up close. "Memorize that mug," I said. "If you see him around here again, go to the office and tell them a pedophile is lurking in the halls."

"What are we going to do now?" asked Abigail.

"Stake-out," I said.

Abigail wasn't entirely happy about the earlier plan to rescue Zania's mom. "D'Arcey, I think we should call the police," she said. "It's getting too dangerous."

"We will. I promise, but I've got to give my plan a shot. It could work."

"When?"

"After school. I've thought about it and I'm going to watch and wait for him to go out. Even if he goes out for cigarettes or something quick, I only need ten minutes tops."

Both Abigail and Kat looked at me as if I were mad. "D'Arcey, you can't do that. It's dangerous. And I can't go with you. I have my music lesson tonight." said Abigail.

"Me neither. I have to babysit," added Kat.

"That's cool. I'll be careful."

Kat and Abigail tried at every opportunity during the rest of the day to talk me out of it, but I was determined.

* * *

The operation called for a serious disguise. I didn't have a lot of time to prepare because I needed to get over to the apartment ASAP. I decided on a bag lady disguise, stuffing a bunch of warm clothes into a big shopping bag. The layers would keep me warm and hide my face. I could change in the subway and pick up a shopping cart at the grocery store to complete my ensemble. Before leaving the house, I told my mother that I was going to help Kat babysit after my shift and that I'd sleep over at Kat's house. Mom wasn't thrilled with the idea and insisted on getting the phone number of the family where Kat was babysitting. I made up a name and a number, then prayed that my mother would have no reason to check up on me. But first, Zania had to take my shift at the restaurant, which meant she needed a miracle cure.

At the restaurant, I found Zania already helping out so I told Mémère the same story I'd told my mother. Anxious to leave, I was detained by Mémère who pulled me into the kitchen.

"Zania is not sick. But she's upset. I know these things. I want to talk to her mother but she keeps putting me off. Tell me the truth, what's going on?"

I pasted on my most sincere-looking face and said in a dramatic whisper, "Mémère, we saw the man at school today. He was looking for Zania."

Mémère gasped and looked around the kitchen door at Zania. "We must call the police. And her mother. Now!"

"No, Mémère. Zania's going home tomorrow. Her mother got a restraining order and it goes into effect at midnight. After that everything is going to be fine. I didn't want to worry you. Mrs. Thomas is going to come here to get Zania and to thank you. Really." Apart from the "really," I was quite convincing. I felt justified in telling the half-truth because I honestly believed that Zania's mom was going to be free of Wayne soon, thanks to me, and that somehow we would convince the police to throw his sorry butt in jail. Forever.

"*D'accord.* I am looking forward to meeting this lady. She has a very nice daughter. But she has very bad taste in men."

"You can say that again," I said. "But not to Zania."

When I was certain Mémère was going to be occupied in the kitchen for a while, I slipped quietly upstairs and changed into my bag lady disguise. Once the sun set, the temperature would drop dramatically and I didn't want to freeze to death in the park. I borrowed a blanket from the linen closet, then filled a grocery bag with fruit, cookies and bottled water.

My bulky garments made me clumsy as I slunk

quietly down the back stairs. Pausing at the bottom, I heard Mémère chatting with Mr. Plawicki. Flipping the deadbolt latch on the backdoor, I stepped into the laneway behind the restaurant. To the left, I saw a couple more stores and then the lane dead-ended at the side wall of a cinder block garage. I walked as quickly as I could in the other direction toward the side street where it always appeared to be brighter than the lane, even in the daylight.

The short hike to Bathurst Street would take too long because I was so awkward lurching about in my bag lady outfit. I decided to take the streetcar, finding a seat near the back. I pulled my hat down low over the black wig and busily examined the hems of the many sweaters and coats I was wearing. In the short time I'd had to get changed, I had raided Mémère's make-up and splotched some dark foundation on my face, trying to make myself look dirty. A quick glance from under my brim reminded me that in Toronto, people never looked at each other on the TTC and they certainly always averted their eyes from homeless people. I was safely anonymous.

Quite a number of riders exited the streetcar at the subway station and each and every one of them shrank away from me like I had cooties. My disguise made me invisible in one sense and threatening in another. At least I was unlikely to be bothered by anyone while I waited in the park. Unless someone called the police. That danger existed. Also, I worried that I might just scare the pants off Zania's mom when I burst through the door, but that was minor.

Although the north end of the platform exited onto Zania's street, I had to shuffle up to the grocery store to borrow a shopping cart. That was likely to be the one instance where I might be challenged. Fortunately, because the carts didn't need a quarter to release them from bondage in the cart park, a number of them sat abandoned throughout the parking lot. I find it amazing how adults will push carts clear across a parking lot in a raging blizzard just to retrieve their 25 cents. When they don't have to deposit a quarter for their carts, they'll leave them anywhere.

I clapped onto a cart which had been abandoned near a hole in the fence that led directly into the yard of the elementary school next door. Strolling nonchalantly across the schoolyard and out the side drive, I cleared store security in a matter of seconds. I took the short walk around to the apartment building. After I arrived, I noticed the Thomas's apartment faced the park where I was going to lurk. A very convenient location when Kat had been trying to film movement at the windows. Now, Wayne had a clear view of me, should he be the kind of guy who gazed out of windows. The park contained few benches, so I had to seat myself on the ground. It felt cold and damp in very short order, so I bought a newspaper from a nearby box to sit on. It helped a little. If the paper became damp through, I had enough change to replace it a few times over.

I'll admit I'm not particularly good at geometry, but I am *acutely* aware of sight angles. Therefore I positioned myself quite close to the building so that, if Wayne happened to look outside, he would be looking down onto the top of my head.

And so began the long night's journey into day. For a kid who lived in front of a television or a computer, the wait stretched out excruciatingly before me. I would say that normally I am extremely focused and attentive, but now I struggled to keep my mind from wandering and my concentration from going with it. All I had to do was keep an eye on the two doors to see Wayne either coming or going. I guessed that Wayne was most likely to exit by the front door because both times I'd seen him, he'd taken the elevator. That told me he didn't use the stairs. And the stairs came out at the side door. So, I made sure to keep my eyes on the front door.

"Oh my God, this is boring," I said, under my breath. Muttering was *de rigueur* for bag ladies, I thought, adding to the credibility of my disguise. Any time someone passed too closely or, surprisingly, looked too closely, I began to mutter and successfully drove the intruder off. "Memo to self," I said into an invisible microphone, "Tell Abigail about opportunity in clothing design — Bag Lady Chic, for people who don't want to be noticed."

Eventually, boredom and muscle cramps forced me to my feet. Taking a chance that I was right about Wayne not taking the stairs, I rolled my cart a short distance down the street, glancing frequently over my shoulder as if being pursued by invisible demons. Then, I turned back, crossed to the other side and wheeled back and forth for a while. Suddenly, I realized that my cart was suspiciously empty with only my small pack and shopping bag, so I acquired some more newspapers. On one of my passes I spied a thrift store donation box in the corner of the park that I hadn't noticed before. It overflowed with donations so I scooted over and filled the cart with clothes and broken bits of kitchen stuff.

A surreptitious glance at my too-shiny watch told me it was nearly 9:00 in the evening. Probably too early for drug dealers to be on the prowl. Although I didn't know anything at all about Wayne's habits, I imagined him to be one of those guys who went out to clubs when most people were coming home from them.

It got too much for me around 11:00. I was tired and cramped, so I pulled off a few layers and stashed them in the cart. Wheeling it around behind the donation box, I took my pack out and walked quickly to the coffee-shop. Thanks to my part-time job and my tips I'm fairly well-financed. And this was one time when the purchase of an insulated mug was not an extravagance. After a necessary "commercial break," I took my new mug filled with hot, black coffee back to the park where I found the cart undisturbed.

Now that it was very dark, I felt safe to sit on the bench. The coffee kept me awake for a while, but at some point, I dozed off. In my dream, I sat on the bench keeping watch. All the apartment windows were dark, the inhabitants fast asleep. The normally busy city was unnaturally quiet so that the blood coursing through my head was the loudest sound I could hear. I stole a glance at Zania's windows at the exact moment a huge spotlight snapped on, illuminating me like I was alone on a huge stage. It was blinding. I could hear Wayne coming even though I couldn't see him. But there was nothing I could do, because not only could I not see, I couldn't move.

My scream was high and thin, more like a squeak, and it woke me up. I tumbled off the bench in a tangle of blanket and clothes, struggling to free myself. Eyes wide open and vision clear, I saw that I was quite alone. Utterly afraid, but knowing it was necessary, I looked up to the fourth floor. It was dark. Confirming that I'd been dreaming, I fought to slow my racing heart and to convince myself not to bolt. I had never been so cold in my life.

The sky became lighter, although clouds kept the colour a lumpy gravy-grey. It was 5:47 a.m. and I had to go to the bathroom again. I didn't want to risk another trip to the coffee-shop so I went behind the donation box. If I could just keep it together a little longer, surely Wayne would go to work. I calculated what time Wayne would have to leave to reach his job in Scarborough. Did he drive? Or take the TTC? I had no clue about the geography of Scarborough. I rarely went anywhere east of Yonge Street. Of course, I also didn't know what time he started work. I got nowhere with all those calculations, but at least it passed the time.

An hour later, with the number of people exiting from the building increasing, I nearly fell off the bench again. The evil blond head bobbed into view. He strode purposefully away up the street toward Bathurst, making me think that he might catch the Bathurst bus, or maybe he parked his car over there. It didn't matter. Thirteen horrible hours on stake-out and I decided to take my chance, come what may. Grabbing my pack, I lurched away from the bench, walking stiffly to the front of the building. Keys in hand, I opened the outside door and nabbed the elevator as the doors were closing.

I would have been happy if the short ride to the fourth floor had lasted a great deal longer. I felt both frightened and excited. Even if Wayne turned around and came right back in behind me, I had time to open the apartment and grab Zania's mom. "I hope he didn't handcuff her to the radiator, or tie her feet. Should have brought bolt cutters," I thought.

I got to the apartment in seconds. With the key already poised in my hand, I grasped the knob and inserted the key into the lock. It went in easily, but wouldn't turn. Puzzled, I pulled it out to check if it was the right one. Of course it was. It had the pink key identifier. Purple for outside, pink for inside. I tried again, still no success. This was an entirely unexpected obstacle. I pounded on the door, calling "Mrs. Thomas! Are you in there?" If Zania's mom was there, she wouldn't or couldn't answer. I was afraid to say my name out loud in case any nosy neighbours ratted me out to Wayne. Frustrated, I stopped pounding and said to the door, "Zania's safe. She's all right. Don't worry."

I heard the sound of a safety chain being unlatched behind me. I ran for the fire exit. Exploding into the open, I fought the impulse to keep running into the safety of the subway. First, I had to retrieve Mémère's blanket and her new coffee mug. Then I took off like a bat out of hell.

Chapter 10

The streetcar started loading when I arrived on the platform. I wanted to ditch some layers of my bag lady outfit before heading to the restaurant, but needed to get out of the area fast. I hopped on the car. At the stop in front of the coffee-shop, people boarded the car carrying hot, steaming cups of coffee that I could smell over the usual stinky streetcar stench. "Soon," I told myself. "Mémère's coffee is waiting." I looked around at the passenger zombies on their unhappy way to jobs they probably hated.

Going along St. Clair took so long that I started to wonder if it wouldn't have been faster to walk. But when my stop finally arrived, I tumbled out of the car on exhausted, wobbly legs and realized that I probably wouldn't have made it more than a block or two. I lurched toward the front door of the restaurant, but when I caught a look at my reflection in a store window, I stared for a moment confused. I'd forgotten about my streetperson disguise. Making a quick 180, I trudged around the block to the alley. Behind the restaurant, I yanked layer after layer of clothes off and piled them on the ground with Mémère's blanket. I could collect them later once I'd made a proper appearance. I wiped off the make-up.

Like a clock winding down, I walked back around, slowing with each step. Through the window, I saw Mémère place a plate of eggs in front of Mr. Plawicki. No sign of Zania. I paused on the sidewalk, waiting for Mémère to return to the kitchen where she would already be working on her lunch specials.

I went inside and went straight to the coffee pot to pour myself a mug of steaming eye-opener. "Hey Mr. Plawicki," I said. "Nice teeth." Recently Mr. Plawicki had been complaining that his false teeth were getting too big. Today he was tucking into his eggs with a shiny new set of choppers. I put down my coffee to pick up the front section of the newspaper. Hit by a huge yawn, I squinted and, on opening my eyes, caught a sight through the window that caused me to drop my paper right into Mr. Plawicki's breakfast.

"Hey," he protested. But I was already gone. My mind raced as fast as my abruptly awakened legs. Would he follow me? Why didn't I have a cellphone of my own? Would he go into the restaurant looking for Zania? Would he hurt Mémère? All this and more churned through my over-active brain before I even got to the back door. I flipped the deadbolt and zipped out the door without a backward glance.

I could only go one way. The sounds of the morning traffic prevented me from hearing if the door had opened behind me. No matter. Adrenaline coursed through me, at least I guess that's what set my feet flying. I ran toward the street with no particular plan in mind other than to lead Wayne away from the restaurant, in case he'd followed me.

Less than ten metres from the end of the lane, I prepared myself to scream my head off if Wayne caught up to me. Five metres now. Straining to hear over the street noise, I started hearing feet pounding behind me, but then again, it could have been my heart. The blood rushed around my brain making a noise like a dozen trains. Three metres. I so wanted to steal a glance behind me, but I couldn't run like a mad thing and look back without falling. I had to slow down anyway or risk running straight out into the street. Taking a chance, I slowed enough to look behind. The alley shimmered in my vision, which was altered by exertion. Nothing. He wasn't following me. Relief.

Now I ran clear of the alley. With an epic gulp of air, I spun south on the sidewalk, right into Wayne's outstretched arms. He clapped his disgusting hand over my mouth, and jerked my head back, nearly ripping it from my body. Something probed into my side. It could have been anything from a finger to a carrot, but under the circumstances I had to assume it was a gun.

The street we were on was a one-way heading north. The few cars passing us approached from behind Wayne, so, unless the drivers looked in their rear-view mirrors, they wouldn't notice anything unusual. He shoved me forward, propelling me around the corner into the lane. Wayne stayed to the south side, keeping us invisible to any motorists passing up the street. I lost hope. Cars almost never came down the lane. You couldn't drive through because of the garage at the end. And it faced onto the next street over. And it wasn't garbage day either.

The laneway, which moments before had seemed infinitely long, now appeared desperately short as Wayne forced me ahead of him toward the restaurant's rear exit. If ever there was a moment in my life to apply what all school-age children had been taught about how to avoid abduction, this was it. But in my panicked state, I couldn't recall the safety rules when being abducted at gunpoint. Flop? Drop? Roll? Pee your pants. I was close, believe me.

Instead, I wriggled about, trying to slow our progress. Wayne's stinky cigarette breath flowed out into my ear. He said one word, "Bang!" and I stopped dead. Then he jabbed the gun painfully into my side. We stood a mere metre from the door. My last hope was to pull Wayne along, past the restaurant door and into the flower shop or the dry-cleaners' further along. But, there on the door, in cheerful white script was a sign — *The Liver Spot*. Any hope that I had that Wayne might be illiterate or stupidly unobservant was dashed when he hissed "Open it."

I wasn't going to give Mémère and Zania up without a fight. I dug in my heels and stood resolute and unmoving at the door. "Listen, kid," said Wayne, "If you want to come out of this alive, open the door." Still I didn't move. I felt a release of pressure in my side. My relief was short-lived, as it was swiftly followed by a violent blow to my head. I saw stars, moon, planets, entire solar systems.

And then, to add insult to injury, Wayne pushed me violently aside and my head crashed into the door-frame on the other side. Even as my knees buckled and I slid to the ground, head screaming and vision blurred, my brain was still firing. I had to warn Mémère and Zania. I struggled to stand, regretting that I hadn't found the time or place to practise my screaming. My mouth opened and I emitted a dry croak. "Mémère!" The effort caused my head to throb so forcefully that I was afraid I'd pass out. Over my head I could hear the sound of heavy footsteps stomping through the apartment. Grasping the handrail, I dragged myself up the stairs.

At the top of the stairs, I had to pull myself onto the landing by reaching around the wall. I flopped on the floor, facing the empty kitchen at the rear of the apartment. On my hands and knees, I crawled painfully into the hall toward the front rooms. And there was Wayne headed back my way. Alone.

He waved the gun at me. "Get up," he said. But the pain in my head got worse from the effort of climbing the stairs and I just about laid down and let Wayne carry on without me. We were like two gunfighters facing each other down in a shoot-out. I really didn't care much at that point if he shot me, because it couldn't be any worse than the shooting pains behind my eyes.

Maybe that's why I barely felt the blow to my side when he booted me out of the way. He stepped over me and raised his foot to kick me again. I pulled my hands up to protect my head. There was a weird sound, like a "splat" and instead of kicking me again, Wayne wobbled off balance. His foot hung the air. I grabbed it and pushed with all my might, tipping him down the stairs. The gun clattered down ahead of him.

I could have stayed there on the landing, cradling my aching head, but I'd seen enough suspense films to know that the bad guys keep popping up like Energizer Bunnies from Hell. The landing grew slippery with blood. I was afraid to look down the stairs, hoping and fearing at the same time that I'd killed him.

Still on the floor, I pulled myself with heavy arms to the edge of the top step and peered down. Wayne lay in a heap on the floor, the entire side of his face smeared with reddish-brown blood. And standing over him with the gun in one hand and a cast-iron frying pan in the other was Mémère. Mindless of the mess on the floor, I put my head down and wept in relief.

I must have passed out briefly, because the next

thing I knew, my head was in Mémère's lap and something cold was pressed against it. "*P'tit chou*," Mémère soothed. "*Ça va, ma fille. Tout va bien.*"

We were still at the top of the stairs, and Wayne was still passed out at the bottom. Instead of Mémère, Mr. Plawicki stood guard, looking quite comfortable wielding the gun. "Polish resistance," said Mémère, reassuringly, "In the war." I managed a tiny smile for Mr. Plawicki who grinned happily at me while aiming the gun at Wayne's head from a cautious distance.

"Zania," I said. "Where's Zania?"

"Next door," replied Mémère. "She was in the kitchen with me when you cried out."

So, I managed to warn them after all. The next minutes hurt my head as sirens screamed up to announce the arrival of the police. They flooded the restaurant making more noise than I would have believed possible. Mémère helped me up off the floor. My hands, clothes and face were sticky. I saw something brown, slimey and hideous resting against the wall. I truly hoped it wasn't Wayne's brains. Or mine. Mémère stooped to pick it up. "Liver," she said. "I told you it was good for you."

If there is a Liver Hall of Fame, that hunk of meat could be the main attraction. Two police officers dragged Wayne out to a squad car. An officer talked to Mémère while a paramedic checked my noggin. So much was going on that my head ached worse, but I pretended I felt fine, in case they decided to take me to the hospital. I wasn't going anywhere until we got Zania's mom back safely. Zania came rushing into the restaurant.

"We need to tell the police about your mom," I said. "Mémère, I need to talk to that policeman, right now!"

Mémère and the police officer looked at me with that "It's okay dear, we've got it all under control" look. I lurched to my feet, grabbing the paramedic for support. Mémère rushed to help. "It's all right, D'Arcey," she said, "I told the officer that that man was here to find Zania. They've taken him away. He can't hurt her now."

"You don't understand," I shouted, or at least that's what it sounded like to me. "He's been holding her mother prisoner. He threatened to hurt her. She may already be ..." I hesitated, seeing a look of horror on Zania's face. I was going to say "dead" but I finished with "hurt," praying that neither was true.

Well, that sure got their attention. Very quickly, I was surrounded by more officers with radios and everyone talked at once. I started to explain but my head was spinning. "You tell them, Zania. I need a time-out." And then the restaurant spun and so did my head.

This time I woke up as they were loading me into an ambulance. I flung my arms out, yelling "Stop!" And they did, looking at me as though I'd just risen from the dead. "I have to go with Zania to find her mother." Mémère hurried over to my side, holding a cordless phone. Behind her, a crowd had gathered and everyone stared at me. A microphone poked through the crowd, aimed in my direction.

I sat up. The stars were gone. The throbbing was receding a bit. Mémère handed the phone to me. "*Ta mère*," she said. I took the phone.

"Hi Mom," I said in my most naturally cheerful voice. Mom was talking a mile a minute on the other end. I guessed she was expressing some concern for my condition but frankly, she wasn't making a heck of a lot of sense. I reassured her. "I'm fine, Mom. No, I don't need to go to the hospital." From the background noise, I could tell my mother was in the car. "I want to go with Zania and the police to get her mother. Please!"

I listened for a while to my mother's objections. "Okay," I said and handed the phone back to Mémère. I turned to find Zania in the crowd, and said, "She'll be here in a few minutes." But what I really wanted to say was "Let's get the heck out of here!"

Mom arrived in a little longer than a few minutes, probably because traffic was stopped in both directions. By that time, I could sit up and the paramedics were off having coffee in the restaurant. Inside, I saw Mr. Plawicki, with a dishtowel tucked into his waistband, serving coffee and nodding cheerfully. My mother had been crying.

"D'Arcey!" was all she said.

"Let's go," I said, looking around for an officer. "Let's get this show on the road. Come on, Zania." I slipped off the gurney and found my legs to be in perfect working order, for the first time that day. I headed for the nearest squad car.

Mémère stopped me. "No, *chèrie*."

"*Oui*, Mémère," I said, firmly. "I'm going."

"D'Arcey you must have your head examined."

"My dad's been saying that for years," I laughed with a wince.

"Then we are coming with you," said Mémère.

She went to the restaurant door and called in to Mr. Plawicki. "Stefan, you keep care of things until I come back, *d'accord*?"

I was right behind her. I needed my pack with the video camera that I'd left on the floor behind the bar. A fair amount of negotiating went on, but then the officer herded Zania, Mémère and me into the back of a car. Anxious to get going, I told the officer at the wheel to "Step on it." He just laughed. Mémère said "Your mother will follow us in the car."

The police cruiser set off at an entirely too-leisurely pace, to my dismay. "Siren, please," I said, tapping on the Plexiglas and making a whirling motion with my finger to illustrate my request.

The officer finally complied, turning on the siren, but they continued to drive too slowly for my taste. Cars pulled aside to let us make the turn at Bathurst and people on the street peered into the car and stared. I waved and turned on the video camera.

Several police cars and another ambulance parked outside Zania's building. The crowd that had gathered on the sidewalk parted, letting our small party through. A policewoman who was on duty outside the building redirected us to the ambulance where paramedics were huddled around a woman swathed in blankets. Zania screeched out "Mommy!" and the woman turned a battered face to us. My heart lurched at the sight of the black, swollen eyes. I switched off the video camera and reached for Mémère's hand. Zania hugged her mother as tears flowed down both their faces.

"D'Arcey, Mémère, come here," Zania called. "Mom, these guys saved my life."

Not exactly. By letting Wayne follow me, I'd come close to getting us all killed.

The paramedics interrupted our reunion and insisted on leaving immediately for the hospital. And Mom insisted on taking me to emergency to have my head examined also. Mom decided that Zania would go with us and that we could go to the same hospital where her mother was being taken. We buckled our seatbelts and Mom started the car. She adjusted the rear-view mirror so that she could see us in the back seat.

"D'Arcey," she said, turning the key in the ignition, "You've got some 'splainin' to do."

Chapter 11

After the ER docs confirmed that I didn't have a skull fracture, we went to the police station to tell the whole story. And then I had to tell it all over again to my parents. Just when it was looking like I was about to be grounded for life, the media started calling. And calling. We made it to the city news. Even the national news called, but my interview was bumped for "breaking news." Most people would be upset about that, but I understand the news business so I was cool. Well, my parents could hardly ground a national hero, could they? Of course, to hear them tell it, I was a national idiot. Parents are so over-dramatic sometimes.

Poor Mémère was so besieged by reporters she had to close the restaurant for a few days just to get away from them. Eventually, the excitement died down and I returned to school. Not just Abigail and Kat, but a whole bunch of students I'm sure I've never even met greeted me as a hero. But the adulation died down as newer stories hit the media and our escapade became yesterday's news.

Although I had been featured in the news, everyone hailed Mémère as the true hero. I was okay with that. *News is not about the reporter.* I spread the newspaper clippings out on the restaurant counter where I was eating fries with Abigail and Kat.

"This is my favourite," I said, holding a front-page item with the headline "Gunman 'meats' his match in liver-wielding Granny." "I wrote that, you know. They came to the house to interview me and I suggested it. The reporter wrote it down. I spelled it out for her, M-E-A-T-S."

Abigail flipped through the clippings. "I don't see anything about the lecture you got from the police."

"Nobody wants to read about that," I said. "What are they going to say? 'Teenager helps nab drug dealer. Gets verbal spanking from parents and police.' I don't think so."

"So, like, are you grounded for life?" asked Kat.

"Of course not," I said. "It's not like I've ever done anything like this before. I mean, what are the chances it'll happen again?" What I meant was, what are the chances I'll get the chance to do it all again? And pay closer attention to what's really going on.

The Liver Spot's popularity increased exponentially, and not just among the neighbourhood pensioners. The old-fashioned bell over the door jingled almost constantly with people seeking meals or just a cup of coffee with the "Meat-packin' Gramma." Another of my quotes.

This time the jingling bell heralded the arrival of a very welcome visitor.

"Zania!" we cried, simultaneously. Our friend stood inside the door, grinning mightily.

After her mom was released from the hospital, Zania had accompanied her to New Brunswick, where she was to recuperate with an aunt in Moncton. They had been away for two whole weeks. During that time, Rhonda's employer had arranged to move them to another apartment in a nearby building. Neither Rhonda nor Zania wanted to stay in their old place with its bad memories and association with Wayne.

We hugged and chattered happily while Mémère stood smiling in the kitchen door. Seeing her, Zania ran to accept a big hug and said, "I'm sorry we deceived you."

"Bah," said Mémère, cheerfully, "It's not your fault. You have nothing to be sorry for." Mémère pointed a finger at me. "But *you*, *ma fille*, you can be sorry until I say different."

"Come on, Mémère. You're loving this. Look at this place," I said, waving my arms to indicate the packed house. "You're getting rich!" Even Mr. Plawicki's photo had been in the paper, and he had presented Mémère with framed copies of all the press clippings for the restaurant walls.

I shoved the plate of fries toward Zania, who

sat on a stool between Abigail and Kat. "How's your new apartment?"

"It's nice. And it's closer to school. And the restaurant."

"Cool," I had actually finagled my way into seeing the apartment and had emailed a report with pictures to Zania in New Brunswick.

"Mémère's giving me a job," said Zania, with a smile in Mémère's direction. It had actually been my idea, which Mémère enthusiastically endorsed. Zania had really taken an interest in cooking and baking when she was staying with Mémère, and with all the extra customers, we truly needed the help.

"Speaking of jobs," said Mémère, tossing a damp cloth at me, "it's time for you to get to work." It was 4:30 and the first wave of early diners would shortly be descending. Zania slid off her stool and grabbed an apron. Mémère put her hand out, "*Non*, Zania," she said. "This is your first night home, you go stay with your *maman*. D'Arcey will work extra hard and give you half her tips."

I made a face at Mémère but nodded to Zania that it was okay with me. She smiled and thanked us both.

"See you tomorrow," I said. Then, I wiped the menu board clean and wrote the evening's specials in my neatest printing. The door opened and in walked Mr. Plawicki wearing a suit with a jaunty hat and a red bow-tie. He bowed grandly and placed a bunch of flowers on the counter.

"For Mémère," he said, before taking his usual

seat. I carried the flowers into the kitchen to find a vase.

"Mémère," I said, with a wicked grin, "Your boyfriend's here."

"Who?" said Mémère, knowing exactly who.

"Pistol Plawicki," I said.

"*Non*," Mémère tried to scowl. "I told you he's my liar. Not my boyfriend." But she couldn't hide her appreciation of the lovely flowers and I swooped out of the kitchen, thinking that love might be in the air.

* * *

After I washed the last pot and closed the blinds, Mémère locked up and joined me at the counter where I was pouring out the dregs of the coffee pot into a china cup.

"It's not good for you, all that coffee," said Mémère.

"I need to stay wide awake. I have homework to do."

"Ha," said Mémère, "Too bad that's decaf."

"What?" I looked back at the coffeemaker and realized it was the orange handled decaffeinated pot I had just emptied. "Oh well, I guess I'll be wide asleep instead."

"So, *mon* D'Arcey. Back to normal life for us."

"Are you kidding, Mémère?"

"No, I'm not. It's back to normal life, no more Detective D'Arcey and men with guns running around in my living room. I'm too old for that kind of excitement."

"Mémère, you're not old!" I retorted. "Why, look at this picture! You don't look a day over 60."

"That's a comfort," said Mémère, drily.

"Were you scared, Mémère?"

"Only for you."

"Me too. I mean, I was just scared for you and Zania."

"Baloney."

"Salami," I said. "I kinda messed up, didn't I?"

Mémère gave me her "*comme çi, comme ça*" head shake.

"I'm sorry. You know, I never meant to put anyone in danger."

She nodded. "You were only trying to help your friend."

"Well, yes, but I guess I was also trying to get a story."

Again, Mémère nodded her head. "It takes more than just the chicken to make soup."

"Huh?"

"Carrots and celery. Rice, a pinch of this and that."

"Mémère, you're getting all Yoda on me."

"If you want to have a tasty soup, you need lots of other ingredients."

My grandmother's story meant I needed to stop trying to be the soup all by myself. And if that wasn't it, well, you figure it out.

I yawned. "Look, the coffee's working already.

The decaf. I'm almost asleep."

"Then go home. You're finished."

"In a while. I like hanging with you."

I needed to do a few things. I hopped off my stool and went to the linen cupboard to set the tables for breakfast. Together, Mémère and I spread the tablecloths, making sure they hung evenly on both sides. While we worked, Mémère asked me about my long-neglected Media Studies project.

"It's kind of hard to go back to dramatizing ancient history once you've found yourself in the middle of a real-life drama, you know?" I said.

"Uh hmmm," replied Mémère, setting out cutlery.

"So I was thinking maybe I'd switch and do a dramatization of our story. I've got lots of footage."

"*Ouais*," said Mémère, handing me some cups and saucers from behind the counter.

"But then I realized that it would be pretty hard for Zania to have to go through it all again, even if it was just a recreation."

"*T'as raison*," said Mémère.

"No thanks," I replied, deliberately misinterpreting my grandmother. "I already ate."

"Hah," said Mémère. Then in a more serious tone she said, "D'Arcey, it is not about you getting a story. It is about things happening to people. You must be careful when dealing with people's lives."

My grandmother sometimes makes me work to figure out what she wants to tell me. I don't know if it's because English isn't her first language or because she wants me to really think about what she's trying say. This was one of those times. "In other words," I said, "It's not about me telling the story. It's who the story is about."

"*Exactement*. Now you understand."

"Mémère, you're a pretty wise old bird. I want to be just like you if I grow up."

"Never happen."

"So, I'm back to Great-uncle Hubert and his speedboat."

Mémère slapped the counter with a napkin. "Bah, Hubert. He was a bad one. Steal the shirt off your back, have it washed at the laundry and send you the bill."

The restaurant was sparkling, ready for the morning. Nothing remained for me to do except give Mémère a great big hug. I pulled on my jacket, picked up my pack and headed for the door. "Mémère," I said, "What do you really think happened to Hubert?"

"I think he stole the money, swam to shore and took a bus to Florida. He hated the winter."

"And lived happily ever after?" I asked.

"Maybe."

"And bought himself a big old Cadillac that he drove around, until he was too shrivelled up to see over the wheel," I said.

"Maybe," said Mémère. "But he didn't buy the car. He stole it."

I laughed in tune with the door chime. "'Night, Mémère!"

At the intersection, I had to wait for the light to change. St. Clair still busted with cars and pedestrians. I glanced back at the restaurant. An old man stopped to check his appearance in the window. He adjusted the angle of his hat and straightened his red bow-tie. The sound of chimes drifted out on the night air as he slipped inside.

The light changed and I stepped into the intersection. "Mémère," I said, out loud, "You rock!"

AGMV Marquis

MEMBRE DE SCABRINI MEDIA

Québec, Canada
2003